The Northern Whale-Fishery

by

Captain Scoresby

The Northern Whale-Fishery
by Captain Scoresby

ISBN: 978-93-64289-96-2

Published by

DOUBLE 9 BOOKS

2/13-B, Ansari Road
Daryaganj, New Delhi – 110002
info@double9books.com
www.double9books.com
Tel. 011-40042856

ABOUT THE AUTHOR

William Scoresby (1789-1857) was a British explorer, scientist, and whaler renowned for his contributions to the understanding of Arctic exploration and the whaling industry during the 19th century. Scoresby received a solid education, particularly in mathematics and natural sciences, laying the groundwork for his later scientific pursuits. Beyond his practical experience, Scoresby was a dedicated scientist and researcher. He conducted numerous scientific experiments and observations during his Arctic expeditions, focusing on meteorology, magnetism, and natural history. Scoresby's scientific contributions were substantial; he made significant advancements in understanding the Earth's magnetic field and was among the first to accurately measure Arctic temperatures and map the region's geography. Scoresby's expertise and scientific rigor earned him recognition among his contemporaries. His writings, including "An Account of the Arctic Regions" and "The Northern Whale-Fishery," became seminal works in Arctic exploration and whaling studies. His detailed accounts of Arctic landscapes, wildlife, and the whaling industry provided valuable insights into the remote and challenging Arctic environment. Throughout his career, Scoresby balanced his roles as a mariner, scientist, and author. He advocated for improved safety measures in the whaling industry and promoted scientific inquiry in maritime exploration. Scoresby's legacy continues to resonate in the fields of Arctic studies and marine science, as his pioneering work laid the groundwork for future explorers and scientists.

William Scoresby's life exemplifies the spirit of exploration and scientific curiosity that defined the 19th-century quest for knowledge in the Arctic. His contributions not only advanced our understanding of polar regions and marine life but also underscored the interconnectedness of scientific inquiry with practical maritime endeavors.

CONTENTS

PREFACE

The following pages are an abridgment, with some modifications and additions, of the second volume of captain (now the rev. Dr.) Scoresby's work on the Arctic Regions and Whale-fishery, Edinburgh, 1820; the substance of the former volume having already appeared in this Monthly Series. The second chapter of the work, on the comparative view of the whale-fisheries of different European nations, has been entirely omitted, as less interesting, it is supposed, to the general reader, than the other chapters.

CHAPTER I
CHRONOLOGICAL HISTORY OF THE NORTHERN WHALE FISHERIES

In the early ages of the world, when beasts of prey began to multiply and annoy the vocations of man, the personal dangers to which he must have been occasionally exposed would oblige him to contrive some means of defence. For this end, he would naturally be induced, both to prepare weapons, and also to preconceive plans for resisting the disturbers of his peace. His subsequent rencounters with beasts of prey would, therefore, be more frequently successful, not only in effectually repelling them when they should attack him, but also, in some instances, in accomplishing their destruction. Hence, we can readily and satisfactorily trace to the principles of necessity the adroitness and courage evidenced by the unenlightened nations of the world, in their successful attacks on the most formidable of the brute creation; and hence we can conceive that necessity may impel the indolent to activity, and the coward to actions which would not disgrace the brave. For man to attempt to subdue an animal whose powers and ferocity he regarded with superstitious dread, and the motion of which he conceived would produce a vortex sufficient to swallow up his boat, or any other vessel in which he might approach it—an animal of at least six hundred times his own bulk, a stroke of the tail of which might hurl his boat into the air, or dash it and himself to pieces—an animal inhabiting at the same time an element in which he himself could not subsist; for man to attempt to subdue such an animal, under such circumstances, seems one of the most hazardous enterprizes of which the intercourse with the irrational world could possibly admit. And yet this animal is successfully attacked, and seldom escapes when once he comes within reach of the darts of his assailer.

It seems to be the opinion of most writers on the subject of the whale-fishery, that the Biscayans were the first who succeeded in the capture of the whale. This opinion, though perhaps not correct, deserves to be mentioned in the outset of an investigation into the probable origin of this employment.

A species of whale, probably the *Balæna rostrata,* was a frequent visitor to the shores of France and Spain. In pursuit of herrings and other small fishes, these whales would produce a serious destruction among the nets of the fishermen of Biscay and Gascony. Concern for the preservation of their nets, which probably constituted the whole of their property, would naturally suggest the necessity of driving these intruding monsters from their coasts. With this view, arrows and spears, and subsequently gunpowder, would be resorted to. Finding the whales timid and inoffensive, the fishers would be induced to approach some individual of the species, and even to dart their spears into its body. Afterwards they might conceive the possibility of entangling some of the species, by means of a cord attached to a barbed arrow or spear. One of these animals being captured, and its value ascertained, the prospect of emolument would be sufficient to establish a fishery of the cetaceous tribe, and lead to all the beneficial effects which have resulted in modern times.

Those authorities, indeed, may be considered as unquestionable, which inform us that the Basques and Biscayans, so early as the year 1575, exposed themselves to the perils of a distant navigation, with a view to measure their strength with the whales, in the midst of an element constituting the natural habitation of these enormous animals; that the English, in 1594, fitted an expedition for Cape Breton, intended for the fishery of the whale and the walrus, (sea-horse,) pursued the walrus-fishing in succeeding years in high northern latitudes, and, in 1611, first attacked the whale near the shores of Spitzbergen; and that the Hollanders, and subsequently other nations of Europe, participated in the risk and advantages of these northern expeditions. Some researches, however, on the origin of this fishery, carried on in the northern seas, will be sufficient to rectify the error of these conclusions, by proving that the whale-fishery by Europeans may be traced as far back at least as the ninth century.

The earliest authenticated account of a fishery for whales is probably that contained in Ohthere's voyage, by Alfred the Great. This voyage was undertaken about 890, by Ohthere, a native of Halgoland, in the diocese of Dronthein, a person of considerable wealth in his own country, from motives of mere curiosity, at his own risk, and under his personal superintendence. On this occasion, Ohthere sailed to the northward, along the coast of Norway, round the North Cape, to the entrance of the White Sea. Three days after leaving Dronthein, or Halgoland, "he was come as far towards the north as commonly the whale-hunters used to travel."

Here Ohthere evidently alludes to the hunters of the walrus, or sea-horse; but subsequently, he speaks pointedly as to a fishery for some species of cetaceous animals having been at that period practised by the Norwegians. He told the king, that with regard to the common kind of whales, the place of most and best hunting for them was in his own country, "whereof some be forty-eight ells of length and some fifty," of which sort, he affirmed, that he himself was one of the six who, in the space of three (two) days, killed threescore.

From this it would appear, that the whale-fishery was not only prosecuted by the Norwegians so early as the ninth century, but that Ohthere himself had personal knowledge of it. The voyage of Ohthere is a document of much value in history, both in respect to the matter of it, and the high character of the author by whom it has been preserved. By a slight alteration in the reading of the Saxon manuscript, as suggested by Turner, in his History of the Anglo-Saxons, it is possible to suppose that the threescore animals slain by Ohthere in two days were not whales but dolphins. This supposition removes the improbability of the exploit recorded, and does not contradict or explain away the fact of larger whales having been likewise hunted and captured.

A Danish work, which there is reason to believe is of a date much earlier than that which we assign to the first fishery of the Basques, declares that the Icelanders were in the habit of pursuing the whales, which they killed on the shore, and that these islanders subsisted on the flesh of some one of the species. And Langebek does not hesitate to assert, that the fishery of the whale (*hovlfangst*, by which he probably means a species of *delphinus*,) was practised in the most northern countries of Europe in the ninth century.

Under the date of 875, in a book entitled the "Translation and Miracles of St. Vaast," mention is made of the whale-fishery on the French coast. In the "Life of St. Arnould, bishop of Soissons," a work of the eleventh century, particular mention is made of the fishery by the harpoon, on the occasion of a miracle said to have been performed by the saint. There are also different authorities for supposing that a whale-fishery was carried on near the coast of Normandy and Flanders, from the eleventh to the thirteenth century.

The English, it is to be expected, did not remain long behind their continental neighbours in this lucrative pursuit. It is difficult to determine whether the whales referred to in the few early documents which we possess, were such as were run on the English shore by accident, or subdued by the English on the high sea. By Acts of Parliament, a.d. 1315 and 1324, the wrecks of whales, cast by chance upon the shore, or whales or great sturgeons *taken* in the sea, were to belong to the king. Henry iv. gave, in 1415, to the church of Rochester, the tithe of the whales taken along the shores of that bishopric. In the sixteenth century, the inhabitants of the shores of the Bay of Biscay were the most distinguished whale-fishers. At first, they confined their attacks to those animals, probably the *Balæna rostrata* of Linnæus, which used to present themselves in the Bay of Biscay at a certain season every year. Gradually becoming bolder, the Biscayans advanced towards the coasts of Iceland, Greenland, and Newfoundland, in the pursuit. The Icelanders united their energies with the Biscayans, and conducted the whale-fishery on so extensive a scale, that, towards the end of the sixteenth century, the number of vessels annually employed by the united nations amounted to a fleet of fifty or sixty sail.

The first attempt of the English to capture the whale, of which we have any satisfactory account, was made in the year 1594. Different ships were fitted out for Cape Breton at the entrance of the Gulf of St. Lawrence, part of which were destined for the walrus-fishery, and the remainder for the whale-fishery. The Grace, of Bristol, one of these vessels, took on board 700 or 800 whale-fins, or laminæ of whalebone, which they found in the Bay of St. George, where two large Biscayan fishermen had been wrecked three years before. This is the first notice I have met with of the importation of this article into Great Britain.

However doubtful it might have appeared at one time whether the English or the Dutch first visited Spitzbergen, the claim of the English to the discovery and first practice of the whale-fishery on the coasts of these islands stands undisputed, the Dutch themselves allowing that the English preceded them four years. The merchants of Hull, who were ever remarkable for their assiduous and enterprizing spirit, fitted out ships for the whale-fishery so early as the year 1598, which they continued regularly to prosecute on the coasts of Iceland and near the North Cape for several years; and after the re-discovery of Spitzbergen by Hudson, in 1607, they were the first to push forward to its coasts. Captain Jonas Poole was, in the year 1610, sent out on a voyage of discovery by the "Company for the Discovery of unknown Countries," the "Muscovy Company," or the "Russia Company," as it was subsequently denominated. On his return, the company fitted out two ships for the fishery; the Marie Margaret, of 160 tons, under the direction of Thomas Edge, factor; and the Elizabeth, of 60 tons, Jonas Poole, master. In this voyage, both ships were lost, but the cargo was brought home in a Hull ship.

Such a novel enterprize as the capture of whales, which was rendered practical, and even easy, by the number in which they were found, and the convenience of the situations in which they occurred—an enterprize at the same time calculated to enrich the adventurers far beyond any other branch of trade then practised—created a great agitation, and drew towards it the attention of all the commercial people of Europe. With that eagerness which men invariably display in the advancement of their worldly interests, but which is seldom directed with equal vigour to objects of higher and eternal importance, the mercantile spirit was concentrated on this new quarter, and vessels from various ports began to be fitted for the fishery. In the next year, three foreign ships made their appearance along with the two belonging to the Russia Company. The English, jealous of the interference of the Dutch, would not allow them to fish, and obliged them to return home. In the following year, the English Russia Company obtained a royal charter, excluding all others, both natives and foreigners, from the fishery, and they equipped seven armed vessels for the purpose of maintaining their prerogative. In the course of the season, the English attacked the foreign vessels, and took from them the greater proportion of the blubber, or oil, and whale-fins, which they had procured, driving them, together with some English ships fitted out by private individuals, out of the country. In 1614, a company was established in Amsterdam, and a charter obtained for three years; ships of war were sent out, and the Hollanders, in defiance of the English, were able to fish without interruption. The English got but half-laden, and the Dutch made but a poor fishing. After various disagreements, and the arrival of the vessels of other powers on the fishing-stations, which tended to divide the quarrel, a conference for the purpose of adjusting their differences ensued between the captains of the rival nations, and they agreed at length to a division of those fine bays and commodious harbours with which the whole coast of Spitzbergen abounded. The English obtained the first choice, and a greater number of bays and harbours than any of the rest. After the English, the Dutch, Danes, Hamburghers, and Biscayans, and, finally, the Spaniards and French, took up their positions. Thus we perceive the origin of the names of the different places called English Bay, Hollanders' Bay, Danes' Bay, etc.

These arrangements having been adopted, each nation prosecuted the fishery in its own possession, or along the sea-coast, which was free for all.

It was understood, however, that the ships of any nation might resort to any of the bays or harbours whatever, for the convenience of awaiting a favourable wind, taking refuge from a storm, or any other emergency. To prevent the prosecution of the fishery in bays belonging to other nations, it was agreed that whenever a boat was lowered in a strange harbour, or happened to row into the same, the harpoon was always to be removed from its rest, so as not to be in readiness for use.

All the early adventurers on the whale-fishery were indebted to the Biscayans for their superintendence and help. They were the harpooners, and the coopers "skilful in setting up the staved cask." At this period, each ship carried two principals; the commander, who was a native, was properly the navigator, as his chief charge consisted in conducting the ship to and from Greenland; the other, who was called by the Dutch, specksynder, or cutter of the fat, as his name implies, was a Biscayan, and had the unlimited control of the people in the fishery, and, indeed, every operation belonging to it was entirely confided to him. When, however, the fishery became better known, the commander assumed the general superintendence, and the specksynder, or specksioneer, is now the principal harpooner, and has the "ordering of the fat," and the extracting or boiling of the oil of the whale, but serves under the direction of the commander.

The Dutch pursued the whale-fishery with more vigour than the English, and with still better effect. It was no uncommon thing for them to procure such vast quantities of oil that empty ships were required to take home the superabundant produce. In 1622, the charter of the Amsterdam Company was renewed for twelve years, and the charter of the Zealand Society was extended about the same time, whereby the latter were allowed to establish themselves in Jan Mayen Island, and to erect boiling-houses and cooperages in common with their associates. The privileges of these companies, occasioning the exclusion of all other persons belonging to the United Provinces, produced a considerable degree of discontent, when the fishery, towards the expiration of these last charters, was in its most flourishing state. The states-general of Friesland were induced to grant a charter to a company formed in that province, which endowed them with similar privileges to those of the other companies of Holland. The Frieslanders, in the year 1634, perceived the advantage of procuring the sanction of the Zealand and Amsterdam companies to their right to participate in the fishery, and after negotiation, the three companies, according to stipulated conditions, contracted a triple union. The Dutch followed the whale-fishery with perseverance and profit, and were successfully imitated by the Hamburghers and other fishermen of the Elbe, but the English made only occasional voyages.

It became apparent to the adventurers in the whale-fishery, that considerable advantages might be realized could Spitzbergen be resorted to as a permanent residence, and they were desirous of ascertaining the possibility of the human species subsisting throughout the winter in this inhospitable climate. The English merchants offered considerable rewards, and the Russia Company procured the reprieve of some culprits who were convicted of capital offences, to whom they promised pardon and a pecuniary remuneration if they would remain a single year in Spitzbergen. The fear of immediate death induced them to comply; but when they were carried out and showed the desolate, frozen, and frightful country they were to inhabit, they shrank back with horror, and solicited to be returned home to suffer death in preference to encountering such appalling dangers. With this request the captain who had them in charge humanely complied, and on their return to England the company interceded on their behalf, and procured pardon.

Probably it was about the same time that nine men, who were by accident separated from one of the London fishing-ships, were left behind in Spitzbergen; all of them perished in the course of the winter, and their bodies were found in the ensuing summer shockingly mangled by beasts of prey. The same master who abandoned these poor wretches to so miserable a fate was obliged, by the drifting of the ice towards the shore, to leave eight of his crew, who were engaged in hunting reindeer for provision for the passage home, in the year 1630. These men, like the former, were abandoned to their fate; for on proceeding to the usual places of resort and rendezvous, they perceived with horror that their own, together with all the other fishing-ships, had departed. By means of the provisions procured by hunting, the fritters of the whale left in boiling the blubber, and the accidental supplies of bears, foxes, seals, and sea-horses, together with the judicious application of the buildings which were erected in Bell Sound, where they took up their abode, they were enabled not only to support life, but even to maintain their health little impaired, until the arrival of the fleet in the following year. It is surely permitted us to hope, that amidst the retirement and dreariness of these frozen regions, these hardy sailors found opportunities for serious reflection and prayer to the God of heaven, and that their minds, with eternity so near to them, were sufficiently acquainted with the one way of salvation to yield themselves to Him who is able to preserve his servants unto life eternal.

The preservation of these men revived in the Dutch the desire of establishing colonies, and in consequence of certain encouragements proclaimed throughout the fleet, seven men volunteered their services, were landed at Amsterdam Island, furnished with the needful articles of provisions, etc., and were left by the fleet on the 30th of August, 1633. About the same time, another party, likewise consisting of seven volunteers, were landed on Jan Mayen Island, and left by their comrades to endure the like painful service with the former. On the return of the fleet in the succeeding year, this last party were all found dead from the effects of the scurvy; but the other, which was left in Spitzbergen, nine degrees further towards the north, all survived. Other seven volunteers proposed to repeat the experiment in Spitzbergen during the ensuing winter, and were quitted by their comrades on the 11th of September, 1634. They all fell victims to the scurvy.

The Dutch, encouraged by the hope that the profitable nature of the whale-fishery would continue unabated, incurred very great expenses in making secure, ample, and permanent erections, which they gradually extended in such a degree that at length they assumed the form of a respectable village, to which, from the Dutch words "smeer," signifying fat, and "bergen," to put up, they gave the name of Smeerenberg. Their expectations of continued success were not, however, justified, and the fishery began to decline so rapidly from the year 1636-7, to the termination of the company's charters, that their losses are stated on some occasions to have exceeded their former profits. On the expiration of the charters, in the year 1642, their renewal was refused by the states-general, and the trade was laid entirely open to all adventurers. It increased in consequence almost tenfold; and on the dissolution of the monopoly, the shipping in the whale-fishery commerce accumulated to between two and three hundred sail. Prior to the time when the trade was laid open, the Jan Mayen whale-fishery, like that of Spitzbergen, attained its maximum. The prodigious destruction of whales occasioned their withdrawal, and the island was at length abandoned as a whale-fishing station.

The whale-fishery of the Dutch was somewhat suspended by the war with England in 1653; but between the years 1660 and 1670, four or five hundred sail of Dutch and Hamburgh ships were yearly visitants to the coasts of Spitzbergen, while the English sometimes did not send a single ship. The British government saw with regret such a profitable and valuable speculation entirely laid aside. To encourage, therefore, its renewal, an Act of Parliament was passed in 1672, whereby the rigours of the Navigation Act were dispensed with, and its essential properties so modified for the ten following years that a vessel for the whale-fishery, being British-built, and having a master and one-half of the crew British subjects, might carry natives of Holland, or other expert fishers, to the amount of the other half. In the year 1693 was formed the "Company of Merchants of London, trading to Greenland," to whom was granted an extension of the indulgences allowed by this Act of Parliament. From various losses, combined, probably, with unskilful management, this company was so unfortunate that, before the conclusion of their term, their capital of £82,000 was entirely expended. These circumstances tended much to discourage the subjects of Great Britain from making any vigorous attempt to renew the fishery. The direct importation of Greenland produce into England being inconsiderable, its importation from Holland or other foreign states was permitted; whalebone, however, was required to be brought into the country in fins only, and not cut, or in any way manufactured; nor could it be landed before the duty chargeable thereon was secured or paid, under penalty of the forfeiture of the goods and double their value. Immense sums were annually paid to foreigners for whalebone at this period.

It was not, it appears, until the whale-fishery was on the decline at Spitzbergen, that the Davis's Strait fishery was resorted to. The Dutch sent their first ships in the year 1719. The shipping employed in the Greenland and Davis's Strait whale-fisheries, in 1721, by foreign nations, amounted to three hundred and fifty-five sail. When, by the lapse of some years, the unfavourable impression produced on the minds of speculative persons by the immense losses suffered by English adventurers in the whale-fishery had partly worn off, the propriety of attempting this trade was suggested by Henry Elking, and was proposed to the directors of the well-known South Sea Company. The British legislature, by exempting the produce of the Greenland Seas from existing duties on the condition of its being imported in British ships, held out encouragements to the company similar to those offered to former adventurers. The South Sea Company caused a fleet of twelve new ships, about 306 tons' burden each, to be built in the river Thames, equipped each vessel with the necessary supplies of cordage, casks, and fishing instruments, and engaged for their use the duke of Bedford's wet-dock at Deptford, where boiling-houses and other conveniences were constructed. In the spring of 1725, the fleet being all in readiness, put to sea, and returned safe with twenty-five and a half whales. The proceeds of this voyage, though scarcely sufficient to pay the expenses incurred by the fitments and the hire of foreign harpooners, were yet superior to those of any succeeding year during the period in which the company pursued the trade. For eight successive years the company persevered in the whale-fishery, with indifferent or bad success, and after the season of 1732 were compelled to abandon it. In 1736, a London ship, which visited the whale-fishery, procured a cargo of seven fish—a degree of success which was fortunately different from that of most of the antecedent English whalers. The English government offered a bounty of twenty shillings per ton on the burden or tonnage of all British whale-fishing ships of 200 tons or upwards; and this, in 1749, was increased to forty shillings per ton.

Gradually the British whale-fishery began to assume a respectable and hopeful appearance. The combined fleets of England and Scotland, in the year 1752, amounted to forty sail; in 1753, to forty-nine; in 1754, to sixty-seven, in 1755, to eighty-two; and in the year following, to eighty-three sail—which was the greatest number of ships employed in the trade for the twenty years following; while the least number amounted to forty sail during the same period. On the establishment of the British whale-fishery, the legislature directed its attention to the means for securing the perpetuity of the trade, and the economical application of the bounty. These enactments were not carried in the House of Commons without considerable debate. In 1768, the king of Prussia, interesting himself in the Greenland fishery, caused some ships to be equipped from Emden; and in 1784, the king of France attempted the revival of the whale-fishery, by equipping, at his own expense, six ships in the port of Dunkirk. In 1785, the king of Denmark, in imitation of the English, granted a bounty of about thirty shillings sterling per ton, to all vessels in the Greenland and Iceland fisheries, on the condition of the ships being fitted out and their cargoes sold in a Danish port.

The Act of the British Parliament of 1786, embodying several additional regulations on the subject of the whale-fishery, and rehearsing and revising former acts, has ever since been considered the fundamental act on the subject of the Greenland and Davis's Strait whale-fishery. By accounts laid upon the table of the House of Commons during this session, it appeared that the bounties granted for the encouragement of the British whale-fisheries, carried on in the Greenland Sea and Davis's Strait, from the year 1733, when bounties were first given, to the end of 1785, had amounted to

£1,064,272. 18*s.* 2*d.* for England, and £202,158. 16*s.* 11*d.* for Scotland. By a subsequent act, the bounty was reduced to twenty-five shillings per ton, from the 25th of December, 1792, to the 25th of December, 1795; and from this period until the expiration of the act in 1798, to twenty shillings per ton, at which latter rate it has continued ever since. From a list, it appears, that in 1788, 255 British ships sailed for the whale-fishery, of which 129 were of a burden under 300 tons; 97 of 300 to 350 tons; 16 of 350 to 400 tons; 11 of 400 to 500 tons; 1 of 565 tons; and 1 of 987 tons. They were fitted out from the ports of London, Hull, Liverpool, Whitby, Newcastle, Yarmouth, Sunderland, Lynn, Leith, Ipswich, Dunbar, Aberdeen, Bo'ness, Glasgow, Montrose, Dundee, Exeter, Whitehaven, Stockton, Greenock, Scarborough, Grangemouth, and Queensferry.

CHAPTER II
SITUATION OF THE EARLY WHALE-FISHERY—THE MANNER IN WHICH IT WAS CONDUCTED—AND THE ALTERATIONS WHICH HAVE TAKEN PLACE

Immediately after the discovery of Spitzbergen by Hudson, in the year 1607, the walrus-fishers, who carried on an extensive and profitable business at Cherie Island, finding the animals of their pursuit become shy and less abundant, extended their voyage to the northward, until they fell in with Spitzbergen, the newly discovered country, about the time when the Russian Company equipped their first ships for the Greenland whale-fishery. As the coast abounded with whales and sea-horses, Cherie Island was deserted, and Spitzbergen became the scene of future enterprize. At this time, the mysticetus was found in immense numbers throughout the whole extent of the coast, and in the different capacious bays with which it abounds. Never having been disturbed, these animals were unconscious of danger; they allowed themselves to be so closely approached that they fell an easy prey to the courageous fishermen. It was not necessary that the ships should cruise abroad, throughout the extended regions of the Polar Seas, as they do at the present time, for the whales being abundant in the bays, the ships were anchored in some convenient situation, and generally remained at their moorings until their cargoes were completed. Not only did the coast of Spitzbergen abound with whales, but the shore of Jan Mayen Island, in proportion to its extent, afforded them in like abundance.

The method used for capturing whales, at this period, was usually by means of the harpoon and lance, though the Dutch inform us that the English made use of nets made with strong ropes for the purpose. The harpoon, which was the instrument used in general practice for effecting their entanglement, consisted, as at present, of a barbed or arrow-shaped iron dart, two or three feet in length, to which was attached a wooden handle, for convenience in striking or throwing it into the whale. Fastened to the harpoon was a line or rope three hundred fathoms in length; more than sufficient to reach the bottom in the bays, where the depth of the water seldom exceeds eighty or one hundred fathoms; so that on a fish descending after being struck, the end of the line could always be detained in the boat. The movements of this boat, of course, corresponded with those of the whale; and so closely pointed out its position, that, on its reappearance at the surface, the other assisting boats were usually very near the place. It was then vigorously pursued, secured by a sufficient number of harpoons, and lastly attacked repeatedly with lances until it was killed.

The lance in use was an iron spear with a wooden handle, altogether ten or twelve feet in length. The capture of the fish, in which, owing to the particular excellence of the situation, they seldom failed, being accomplished, it was towed by the boats, rowing one before another "like a team of horses," to the ship's stern, where it lay untouched from one to two or three days. The fat being then removed was carried to the shore, where ample conveniences being erected, it was afterwards subjected to heat in a boiler, and the greater part of the oil extracted.

As the usual process of the early fishers for extracting the oil may be interesting to some readers, I shall attempt to describe it, following the accounts by captains Anderson and Gray, whose papers are preserved among the manuscripts in the British Museum.

The blubber being made fast to the shore, a "waterside man," standing in a pair of boots, mid-leg in the sea, flayed off the fleshy parts, and cut the blubber into pieces, of about two hundred weight each. Two men, with a barrow, then carried it, piece by piece, to a stage or platform, erected by the side of the works, where a man, denominated a "stage-cutter," armed with a long knife, sliced it into pieces, one and a half inches thick, and about a foot long, and then pushed it into an adjoining receptacle, called a "slicing cooler." Immediately beyond this cooler, five or six choppers were arranged in a line, with blocks of whales' tails before them; and adjoining these blocks was another vessel, called a "chopping cooler," of two or three tons' capacity. These men, being situated between the two coolers, took the sliced blubber from the slicing cooler, and, after reducing it into little bits, scarcely one-fourth of an inch thick, and an inch or two long, pushed it into the chopping cooler. These operations were carried on as near as convenient to the place where the copper was erected.

The copper held only half a ton. It was furnished with a furnace, and the requisite appendages. A man, designated "tub-filler," with a ladle of copper, was employed in filling a hogshead with chopped blubber, dragging it to the copper, and emptying it in, until the copper was full. A fire of wood was, in the first instance, applied, but after a copper or two had been boiled, the finks or fritters were always sufficient to boil the remainder without any other fuel. When the blubber was sufficiently boiled, two men, called "copper men," with two long-handled copper ladles, took the oil and finks out of the copper, and put it into a "fritter barrow," which, being furnished with a grating of wood in place of a bottom, drained the oil from the fritters, from whence it ran into a wooden tank or cooler, of about five tons' capacity. Three coolers were usually provided, and placed some feet asunder, a little below each other; a quantity of water was put into each before the oil, and the oil, whenever it came to a certain height in the first cooler, escaped through a hole, by a spout, into the second, the same way into the third, and from thence, by a plug-hole, into the casks or butts in readiness for its reception. When the oil in these butts was thoroughly cold, whatever it had contracted was filled up, and the casks then rolled into the water, and, in rafts of twenty together, were conveyed into the ship.

The whalebone was separated from the gum, or substance in which it is imbedded, rubbed clean, packed in bundles, of sixty laminæ or blades each, and taken to the ship in the longboat. Thus prepared, the cargo was conveyed home, either when a sufficiency was procured, or the close of the season put an end to the fishing occupations. While some of the people belonging to the whale-ships were engaged in boiling the blubber, the rest of the crew, it is probable, were occasionally employed in the capture of other whales. Besides the buildings made use of in boiling the blubber, the whale-fishers had other buildings on shore for lodging the blubber-men in, and for the use of the coopers employed in preparing the casks.

So long as the whales remained in the immediate vicinity of the fishing establishments, the boats were sent out of the bay, the fish captured at sea, towed into the harbour, stripped of the fat, and the blubber boiled in the manner described; but as the whales increased their distance, this plan of procedure became inconvenient, so that the ships began to cruise about the sea, to kill the whales wherever they found them, to take on board the blubber, and only occasionally to enter a port. So far now from having occasion for empty ships for carrying away the superabundant produce, it was a matter of difficulty and uncertainty to procure a cargo at all; and, with the most prosperous issue, there was not sufficient time for landing the cargo and extracting the oil; the blubber was therefore merely packed in casks and conveyed home, where the remaining operations of extracting the oil, and cleaning and preparing the whalebone, were completed. Hence, the various buildings, which had been erected at a great expense, became perfectly useless; the coppers, and other apparatus that were worth the removal, were taken away, and the buildings of all the different nations, both at Spitzbergen and at Jan Mayen Island, were either wantonly razed to the ground, or suffered to fall into a state of decay.

When the whales first approached the borders of the ice, the fishers held the ice in such dread, that whenever an entangled fish ran towards it, they immediately cut the line. Experience, through time, inured them to it; occasionally they ventured among the loose ice, and the capture of small whales at fields was at length attempted, and succeeded. Some adventurous persons sailed to the east side of Spitzbergen, where the current, it is believed, has a tendency to turn the ice against the shore; yet here, finding the sea, on some occasions, open, they attempted to prosecute the fishery, and, it seems, with some success, a great whale-fishery having been made near Stansforeland, in the year 1700. The retreat of the whales from the bays to the sea-coast, thence to the banks at a distance from land, thence to the borders of the ice, and finally to the sheltered situations afforded by the ice, appears to have been fully accomplished about the year 1700, or from that to 1720. The plan of prosecuting the fishery now underwent a material change, especially in reference to the construction of the ships, and the quality and quantity of the fishing apparatus.

When the fishery could be effected entirely in the bay, or even along the sea-coast, any vessels which were sea-worthy, however old or tender, were deemed sufficient to proceed to Spitzbergen, and were generally found adequate to the purpose, especially as they did not set out till the spring was far advanced, thereby avoiding obstructions from the ice and from sudden and destructive storms. When, however, the fishing had to be pursued in the open sea, new, or at least very substantial ships, became requisite, and even these it was found necessary to strengthen on the bows and stern, and on the sides, by additional planks. A greater quantity of fishing-stores also became needful. When fishing among the ice, the whales, after having been struck, frequently penetrated to a great distance out of the reach of their assailants, dragging the line away, until at length they found it necessary to cut it to prevent further loss. Hence, by the frequency of disasters among their ships, the increased expense of their equipment, and the liability of losing their fishing-materials, such an additional expense was occasioned as required the practice of the most rigid economy to counterbalance it. The destruction of the shipping by the ice, in the Dutch fleet alone, was frequently near twenty sail in one year, and on some occasions above that number. The Greenland men of the present day being mostly ice-fishers, an account of the improved mode of fishing now practised will be sufficient for the illustration of the method followed by the Dutch and other nations at a more early period, particularly as the way in which the whale is pursued and killed is pretty nearly the same at this time as it was a hundred years ago.

Davis's Strait, or the sea lying between the west side of Old Greenland and the east side of North America, and its most northern islands, has generally, since the close of the seventeenth century, been the scene of an advantageous whale-fishery. This fishery was first attempted by the Dutch, in 1719; after which period it was usually resorted to by about three-tenths of their whalers, while seven-tenths proceeded to Spitzbergen. This fishery differs only from that of Spitzbergen or Greenland, in the sea being, in many districts, less incommoded with ice, and in the climate being somewhat more mild. The alterations which have taken place in it are, in some measure, similar to those which have occurred at Spitzbergen. The fish which, half a century ago, appear to have resorted to all parts of the western coast of Old Greenland, in a few years retired to the northward, but they still remained about the coast. Of late, however, they have deserted some of the bays which they formerly frequented, and have been principally caught in icy situations in a high latitude, or in the opening of Hudson's Strait, or at the borders of the western ice, near the coast of Labrador.

Baffin's Bay was suggested as an excellent fishing-station, by the voyager whose name it bears, so early as the year 1616, when his memorable navigation was performed. Baffin, in a letter addressed to J. Wostenholm, esq., observes, that great numbers of whales occur in the bay, and that they are easy to be struck; and, though ships cannot reach the proper places until toward the middle of July, "yet they may well tarry till the last of August, in which space much business may be done, and good store of oil made." To this situation, where the whales have never been molested until recently, it appears they still resort in the same manner, and in similar numbers, as in the time of Baffin. In 1817, two or three of the Davis's Strait whalers proceeded through the strait into Baffin's Bay, to a much greater length than they were in the habit of adventuring, where, in the months of July and August, they found the sea clear of ice, and in some parts abounding with whales. A Leith ship, which, it appears, advanced the furthest, made a successful fishery in lat. 76°-77°, after the season when it was usual for ships to depart. This fact having become generally known, several other ships followed the example, in the season of 1818, and persevered through the barrier of ice lying in 74°-75° towards the north. After they had succeeded in passing this barrier, they found, as in the preceding year, a navigable sea, where several ships met with considerable success in the fishery, at a very advanced period of the season. This discovery is likely to prove of great importance to the fishery of Davis's Strait. Ships, which fail of success in the old stations, will still, in the new fishery, have a reserve of the most promising character. Hence, instead of this fishery being necessarily closed in July, the period when the whales have usually made their final retreat from the old fishing-stations, it will in future be extended to the end of August at least; and it may ultimately appear that there will be little danger of ships being permanently frozen up, unless previously beset in the ice during any part of the month of September.

CHAPTER III
ACCOUNT OF THE MODERN WHALE-FISHERY, AS CONDUCTED AT SPITZBERGEN

We commence this chapter with a description of a well-adapted Greenland ship, and of the manner in which it should be strengthened to resist the concussions of the ice. A ship intended for the Greenland or Davis's Strait trade, should be of three or four hundred tons' admeasurement, very substantially built, doubled, and fortified; should have six or seven feet perpendicular space between decks; should be furnished with a description of sails which are easily worked; and should possess the property of fast sailing. The most appropriate dimensions of a ship intended for the northern whale-fisheries, seems to be that which is so large as to be capable of deriving the greatest advantage from the best opportunity, and no larger. A vessel of 250 tons requires nearly the same number of men, the same quantity of provisions and stores, and the same expense of outfit, as a ship of 350 tons' burden; while the difference in the cargoes of the two vessels when filled, is in one voyage more than a compensation for the difference in the first expense. Besides, for want of similar room and convenience, the smaller ship has not always an equal chance of succeeding in the fishery with the larger. And, as ships of about 350 tons' burden have been occasionally filled, vessels of 250 tons are too small for the fishery. Ships of 350 tons' burden have, we observe, been occasionally filled, but we know of no instance in which a ship of 400 tons, of the usual capacious build, has been deficient in capacity for taking in as large a cargo as of late years there has been any opportunity of procuring. We therefore conclude, that an increase of dimensions above 400 tons is an actual disadvantage, and that a ship of intermediate size, between 300 and 400 tons, is best adapted for the fishery.

Greenland ships, in the early ages of the fishery, were very indifferent structures, and even of late shipping of inferior quality were generally deemed sufficient for the trade. At present, however, when a good fishery is rarely made without frequent exposure to the ice, and sometimes in very critical situations, the vessels require to be substantially built, for the purpose of resisting the occasional pressure of, and frequent blows from, the ice, to which the ships of persevering fishermen must always be more or less exposed. The requisites peculiar to a Greenland ship, the intention of which is to afford additional strength, consist of doubling, and sometimes trebling, and fortifying. The terms "doubling" and "trebling," are expressive of the number of layers of planks, which are applied to the exterior of a frame of timbers; hence, a ship which has one additional series of planks, is said to be doubled, and such ships as are furnished with two, or part of two, additional layers of planks, are said to be trebled. Doubling generally consists of the application of two or two half inches oak plank, near the bow, diminishing towards the stern to perhaps half that thickness, and extending in one direction from the lower part of the main-wales, to within six feet perpendicular of the keel forward, and to within eight or nine feet abaft; and, in the other direction, that is, fore and aft-wise, from the stem to the stern-post. Doubling is used for producing an increase of strength, and at the same time for preserving the outside or main planks of the ship from being injured by the friction of passing ice. Trebling, which commonly consists of one and a half to two inches oak plank, is generally confined to the bows of the ship, and rarely extends farther aft than the fore-chains or chesstree. It is seldom applied but to second-rate ships. Its principal use is to increase the strength of the ship about the bows, but it also, serves to preserve that part of the doubling which it covers from being destroyed by the ice.

Fortifying is the operation of strengthening a ship's stern and bows by the application of timber and iron plates to the exterior, and a vast number of timbers and stanchions to the interior. Four straight substantial oak timbers, called ice-beams, about twelve inches square and twenty-five feet in length, are placed beneath the hold-beams, butting with their foremost extremity against a strong fore-hook, and extending nearly at right angles across three or four of the hold-beams, into each of which they are notched and secured, at the point of intersection, by strong iron bolts, with the addition of "cleats" on the aftermost-beams. The fore-part of the ice-beams, which butt against the hook, are placed at a small distance from each other, from whence they diverge in such a way that their other extremities divide the aftermost beams under which they pass into five equal parts. The next important part of the fortification is the *pointers*, which consist of four or more crooked timbers, fitting the curve of the ship's bow on each side; these are placed below the hold-beams, against the inside of the ceiling, nearly parallel with the direction of the planks, some butting against the fore-hooks, and others passing between them. Across these pointers, four or five smaller timbers, called "riders," disposed at regular distances, are placed at right angles, that is, in the same direction as the ribs of the ship. Now, from each of the points of intersection of the riders and pointers, consisting of eighteen or twenty on each side of the ship, a stanchion, or shore, proceeds to the edge of one of the two ice-beams, placed on the same side, where it is secured in a rabbet. The ice-beams are supported and connected by several strong pieces of wood, placed between each two, in different parts, called "carlings," whereby they are made to bear as one. It is evident that a blow received on the starboard-bow will be impressed on the adjoining pointers, and the impression communicated, through the medium of the lateral timbers, or shores, to the two ice-beams on the same side, thence by the carlings to the other ice-beams, and then, by the shores on the opposite side to the larboard-bow and annexed pointers. A blow cannot be received on any part of one bow, without being communicated by the fortification to every part of the opposite bow, while every part to and through which the impression is communicated must tend to support that place on which the blow is impressed.

To preserve the stem from being shattered or bruised by direct blows from the ice, it is strengthened by an extra piece called the false, or ice-stem. On the side of this are placed the ice-knees, which are angular chocks, or blocks of wood, filling the concavity formed by the stem and bow planks, and extending from about the eight feet mark to the loading mark. In the best style, the ice-knees are twelve to fifteen inches in thickness at the stem, diminishing to, perhaps, six or eight inches thick at the distance of about eight feet from the stem, from thence gradually becoming thinner, until they fall into and incorporate with the common doubling, below the fore-part of the fore-chains. This makes a neat bow, and in point of strength is much preferable to the angular chocks or knees, which usually extend about five or six feet from the stem, and then terminate somewhat abruptly upon the doubling. Ice-knees not only strengthen the front of the bows, and prevent the main planks from being bruised or shattered, as far as they extend, but likewise protect the stem from the twisting effect of a side blow. The stem and the small part of the ice-knees adjoining, are still farther defended by plates of half-inch iron, called ice-plates, which are nailed upon the face of the ice-stem, and partly on the ice-knees, to prevent them being cut by the ice.

For additional strength, as well as convenience, the hold-beams of a Greenland ship should be placed low, or at a greater distance from the deck-beams than is usual in other merchantmen, leaving a clear space of six or seven feet between decks. The strength thus derived is principally serviceable when the ship is squeezed between two sheets of ice; because the nearer the pressure acts on the extremities of the beams, the greater is the resistance they are calculated to offer. A large space between decks is found also, for many reasons, to be most convenient.

Hammocks, as receptacles for sailors' beds, being incommodious, the crew are lodged in cabins or berths, erected in the half-deck; these consist of twelve to twenty in number, each of which is calculated to contain two or three persons. When a ship is on fishing-stations, the boats are required to be always ready for use; as such they are suspended from cranes, fixed on the sides of the ship, and are usually so contrived that a boat can be lowered down into the water, manned, and pushed off from the ship, in the short space of a minute of time. Prior to the year 1813, a ship having seven boats carried one at each waist, that is, between the main-mast and fore-mast, two at each quarter, one above the other and one across the stern. An improvement on this plan, adopted in 1813, is to have the boats fixed in a line of three lengths of boats on each side.

The masts and sails of a Greenland vessel are not without their peculiarities. As it is an object of importance that a fishing-ship should be easily navigated, under common circumstances, by a boat's crew of six or seven men, it is usual to take down royal masts, and even top-gallant masts, and sometimes to substitute a long light pole in place of a mizen top-mast; also, to adopt such sails as require the least management. Courses set in the usual way require a number of men to work them when the ship is tacked; a course, therefore, made to diminish as it descends, that is, narrowest at the foot or lower part, and extended by a boom, or yard below as well as above, and this boom fastened by a tackle fixed at its centre to the deck, swings with the yards, with little or no alteration, and is found particularly convenient. Fore-sails, on this principle, have been in use about six or seven years. In 1816, I fitted a main-sail or cross-jack, in the same way, the former of which we found of admirable utility. Boom-courses are not only convenient in tacking, but are likewise a valuable acquisition when sailing among crowded dangerous ice. As the safety of the ship depends, next to the skilfulness of the piloting officer, on a prompt management of the yards and sails, boom-courses are strikingly useful on account of the little attention they require when any alteration in the position of the sails becomes necessary; and when the ship's head-way is required to be suddenly stopped in a situation where she cannot be luffed into the wind, boom-courses swinging simultaneously with the top-tails are backed without any annoyance from tacks or sheets, and of course assist materially in effecting the intention. Such is the advantage of this description of sails, that on one occasion, when all the rest of my crew were engaged in the capture of a whale, with the assistance of only two men, neither of them sailors, I repeatedly tacked a ship of 350 tons' burden under three courses, top-sails and top-gallant sails, together with jib and mizen, in a strong breeze of wind. Gaf-sails between the masts, in the place of stay-sails, are likewise deservedly in much repute. To the mizen and try-sail, or gaf main-sail, that have been long in use, I have added a gaf fore-sail of similar form, besides which, my father has also adopted gaf top-sails between each mast. These sails produce an admirable effect when a ship is "on a wind," which is the kind of sailing most required among the ice.

Having now described a Greenland ship, it is time to detail the proceedings on board of her, from putting to sea to her arrival on the coast of Spitzbergen. When all necessary conditions have been fulfilled, and the ship cleared out at the custom-house, the first opportunity is embraced for putting to sea. This is generally accomplished in the course of the month of March, or at least before the tenth of April. The crew of a whale-ship usually consists of forty to fifty men, comprising several classes of officers, such as harpooners, boat-steerers, line-managers, carpenters, coopers, etc., together with fore-mast men, landmen, and apprentices. As a stimulus to the crew in the fishery, every individual, from the master down to the boys, besides his monthly pay, receives a gratuity for every size fish caught during the voyage, or a certain sum for every tun of oil which the cargo produces. Masters and harpooners, in place of monthly wages, receive a small sum in advance before sailing, and if they procure no cargo whatever, they receive nothing more for their voyage; but in the event of a successful fishing, their advantages are considerable. The master usually receives three guineas for each size fish, and as much for striking a size whale or discovering a dead one, together with ten shillings to twenty shillings per tun on oil, and commonly a thirtieth, a twenty-fifth, or a twentieth of the value of the cargo besides. He also has about £5 per month for his attendance on the ship while he remains on shore. Each harpooner has usually 6s. per tun on oil, together with half a guinea for every size fish he may strike during the voyage. In addition to which the chief-mate, who is generally also harpooner, has commonly two guineas per month when at sea, and a guinea for each size fish. The specksioneer, or chief-harpooner, has also half a guinea per fish, and sometimes a trifle per tun of oil additional; and the second-mate, and other officers who serve in a compound capacity, have some additional monthly wages. Boat-steerers, line-managers, and fore-mast-men, commonly receive about 1s. 6d. per tun each, besides their monthly pay, and landmen either a trifle per tun on oil, or a few shillings for each size fish.

From the difference in the wages paid in different ports, it is not easy to say what is the amount received by each class of officers belonging to the whale-ships. In the general, however, it may be understood that, on a ship with 200 tuns of oil, which is esteemed an excellent cargo, the chief-mate receives about £95 for his voyage, a harpooner about £70, and a common sailor, or foremast-man, about £25. including advance money and monthly pay. As the master's wages depend as much on the value of the cargo as upon its quantity, it is difficult to give an opinion as to the amount; generally speaking, however, with a cargo of 200 tuns of oil, he will receive about £250 or £300, when his pay is according to the lowest scale; and perhaps £500 or £600, or upwards, when he is paid after the highest rate.

In time of war, the *manning* of the whale-ships at the ports where they were respectively fitted out being sometimes impracticable, and always a matter of difficulty, it was usual for the owners and masters of such ships to avail themselves of the privileges allowed by act of parliament of completing their crews in Shetland and Orkney. These islands were, therefore, the frequent resort of most of the fishermen; those bound for Spitzbergen commonly put into Shetland, and those for Davis's Strait into Orkney. But in the present time of peace, also, several ships, in consequence of the higher wages demanded by the English seamen, have availed themselves of a late extension of the act for permitting a certain amount of extra men to be taken on board in Shetland or Orkney, during the continuance of the bounty system.

In Shetland, it is usual for the fishermen to *trim* their ships, and complete their ballast, by filling most of their empty casks with water, where it has not previously been done, to replenish their fresh water, to lay in stocks of eggs, fish, fowls, sea-sand, etc., to divest the ships of all elevated lumber and gaudy appendages to the masts and rigging, by way of preparing them for enduring the Polar storms with greater safety and convenience, and lastly, to fix a "crow's nest" or "hurricane house," on the mast of each ship, and prepare a passage to it as safe and convenient as possible.

The "crow's nest" is an apparatus placed on the main top-mast, or top-gallant mast-head, as a kind of watch-tower for the use of the master or officer of the watch in the fishing-seas, for sheltering him from the wind, when engaged in piloting the ship through crowded ice, or for obtaining a more extensive view of the sea around when looking out for whales. When sailing among much drift-ice, as seen from the deck, it seems at a small distance impervious, although it may happen that scarcely any two pieces are connected; but from the mast-head, the relative position of almost every piece may be distinctly seen, and an opinion may be formed by the experienced observer of the probable and actual movements of such pieces as the ship is required to pass. This is an object of the greatest importance, because the varied movements of the different pieces occasion such an alteration in the channel pursued, that, were it not for a constant, attentive, and judicious watch by the master or an able officer, a ship would not pass through any crowded collection of drift-ice without the imminent risk of being stove.

In difficult situations, a master's presence at the mast-head is sometimes required for many hours in succession, when the temperature of the air is from 10° to 20° below the freezing point, or more. It is therefore necessary for the preservation of his health, as well as for his comfort, that he should be sheltered from the piercing gale. A piece of canvas tied round the head of the main top-mast, and heel of the top-gallant mast, extending only from the cap to the cross-trees, or at best, a canvas stretched round the base of the top-gallant rigging, but open on the after-part, was the most complete contrivance of a crow's nest, until a few years ago my father invented an apparatus, having the appearance of a rostrum, which afforded an admirable defence against the wind. This contrivance, from the comfortable shelter it affords to the navigator, having come into very general use, it may not be improper to describe it more particularly.

The one most approved by the inventor is about four and a half feet in length, and two and a half in diameter. The form is cylindrical, open above and close below. It is composed of laths of wood, placed in a perpendicular position, round the exterior edge of a strong wooden hoop, forming the top, and round a plane of mahogany or other wood which forms the bottom, and the whole circumference of the cylinder is covered with canvas or leather. The entrance is by a trap-hatch at the bottom. It is fixed on the very summit of the main top-gallant mast, from whence the prospect on every side is unimpeded. On the after-side is a seat, with a place beneath for a flag. In other parts are receptacles for a speaking-trumpet, telescope, and occasionally for a rifle-piece, with utensils for loading. For the more effectual shelter of the observer, when in an erect posture, a movable screen is applied to the top on the windward side, which increases the height so much as effectually to shield his head. When the ship is tacked, nothing more is necessary for retaining the complete shelter than shifting the screen to the opposite side, which is done in an instant.

The Greenland ships usually leave Shetland towards the end of March, or the beginning of April. From thence, if their view be to avail themselves of the benefit of the seal-fishery, they steer to the northward, on the meridian, or a little to the westward, and commonly make the ice in the latitude of 70° to 72° north. But if the month of April be much advanced before they leave Shetland, they generally steer for the whaling-stations on a course to the east of north, with the view of falling into that remarkable indentation of the Polar ice, lying in 5° or 10° east longitude, which I have denominated the "Whale-Fishers' Bight." It used to be the practice to remain on sealing-stations until the beginning of May, and not to enter the ice until about the middle of the month; but of late it has become usual to push into the ice at a much earlier period, though the practice is neither without its dangers nor disadvantages. If a barrier of ice prevents the fisher from reaching the usual fishing-station, he sometimes perseveres in search of whales on the southward margin of the ice, but more generally endeavours to push through it into an opening, which is usually formed on the west side of Spitzbergen, in the month of May, where he seldom fails of meeting with the objects of his search. It is a common remark, that the more difficulty there is attending the passage through the ice, the better is the fishery when that passage is accomplished. In close seasons, very few ships pass the barrier before the middle or end of May. Those which first succeed immediately proceed along the edge of the western ice to the latitude of 78° or 79°, until they meet with whales. But in open seasons, the most recommendable plan is to sail direct to the latitude of 80°, when it can be accomplished at a very early period, where large whales are generally at this season to be found.

It is not yet ascertained what is the earliest period of the year in which it is possible to fish for whales. The danger attending the navigation amidst massive drift-ice, in the obscurity of night, is the most formidable objection against attempting the fishery before the middle of the month of April, when the sun, having entered the northern tropic, begins to enlighten the Polar regions throughout the twenty-four hours. Some ships have sailed to the northward of the 78th degree of latitude, before the close of the month of March; but I am not acquainted with a single instance where the hardy fishers have, at this season, derived any compensation for the extraordinary dangers to which they were exposed. In the course of the month of April, on certain occasions, considerable progress has been made in the fishery, notwithstanding the frequency of storms. At the first stage of the business, in open seas, the whales are usually found in most abundance on the borders of the ice, near Hackluyt's Headland, in the latitude of 80°. A degree or two further south they are sometimes seen, though not in much plenty; but in the 76th degree they sometimes occur in such numbers, as to present a tolerable prospect of success in assailing them.

Some rare instances have occurred wherein they have been seen on the edge of the ice, extending from Cherie Island to Point Look-out, in the early part of the season. Grown fish are frequently found at the edge, or a little within the edge, of the loose ice, in the 79th degree of north latitude, in the month of May; and small whales, of different ages, at fields, and sometimes in bays of the ice, in the 80th degree. Usually the fish are most plentiful in June, and, on some occasions, they are met with in every degree of latitude from 75° to 80°. In this month, the large whales are found in every variety of situation; sometimes in open water, at others in the loose ice, or at the edges of fields and floes, near the main impervious body of ice, extending towards the coast of West Greenland. The smaller animals of the species are, at the same time, found further to the south than in the spring, at floes, fields, or even among loose ice, but most plentifully about fields or floes, at the border of the main western ice, in the latitude of 78° or 78½°. In July, the fishery generally terminates, sometimes at the beginning of the month, at others, though more rarely, it continues throughout the greater part of it. Few small fish are seen at this season.

The parallel of 78° to 78½° is, on the whole, the most productive fishing-station. The interval between this parallel and 80°, or any other situation more remote, is called the "northward," and any situation in a lower latitude than 78° is called the "southward." Though the 79th degree affords whales in the greatest abundance, yet the 76th degree affords them, perhaps, more generally. In this latter situation a very large kind of the mysticetus is commonly to be found, throughout the season, from April to July inclusive. Their number, however, is not often great; and as the situation in which they occur is unsheltered, and, consequently, exposed to heavy swells, the southern fishery is not much frequented. The parallel of 77° to 77½° is considered a "dead latitude" by the fishers, but occasionally it affords whales also.

From an attentive observation of facts, it would appear that various tribes of the mysticetus inhabit different regions, and pursue various routes on their removal from the places where first seen. These tribes seem to be distinguished by a difference of age or manners, and, in some instances, apparently by one of species or subspecies. The systematical movements of the whales receive illustration from many well-known facts. Sometimes a large tribe, passing from one place to another, which, under such circumstances, is denominated a "run of fish," has been traced in its movements, in a direct line from the south towards the north, along the seaward edge of the western ice, through a space of two or three degrees of latitude; then it has been ascertained to have entered the ice, and penetrated to the northward beyond the reach of the fishers. In certain years, it is curious to observe, that the whales commence a simultaneous retreat throughout the whole fishing limits, and all disappear within the space of a very few days.

Having now mentioned, generally, the principal places resorted to by the whales in the Spitzbergen seas, it will, possibly, be interesting to such as are in any way concerned in the fishery, to notice more distinctly their favourite haunts under particular circumstances.

Experience proves that the whale has its favourite places of resort, depending on a sufficiency of food, particular circumstances of weather, and particular portions and qualities of the ice. Thus, though many whales may have been seen in open water when the weather was fine, after the occurrence of a storm perhaps not one is to be seen; and, though fields are sometimes the resort of hundreds of whales, yet, whenever the loose ice around separates entirely away, the whales quit them also. Hence, fields seldom afford whales in much abundance, excepting at the time when they first "break out," and become accessible; that is, immediately after a vacancy is made on some side by the separation of adjoining fields, floes, or drift-ice. Whales are rarely seen in abundance in the large open spaces of water which sometimes occur amidst fields and floes, nor are they commonly seen in a very open pack, unless it be in the immediate neighbourhood of the main western ice. They seem to have a preference for close packs and patches of ice, and for fields under certain circumstances; for deep bays, or *bights*, and sometimes for clear water situations; occasionally for detached streams of drift-ice, and most generally for extensive sheets of bay-ice. Bay-ice is a favourite retreat of the whales, so long as it continues sufficiently tender to be conveniently broken for the purpose of respiration. In such situations, whales may frequently be seen in amazing numbers, elevating and breaking the ice with their crowns, the eminences on their heads in which their blow-holes are situated.

The most favourable opportunity for prosecuting the fishery commonly occurs with north, north-west, or west winds. At such times, the sea near the ice is almost always smooth, and the atmosphere, though cloudy and dark, is generally free from fog or thick snow. The fishers prefer a cloudy to a clear sky, because, in very bright weather, the sea becomes illuminated, and the shadows of the whale-boats are so deeply impressed in the water by the beams of the sun, that the whales are very apt to take the alarm, and evade the utmost care and skill of their pursuers. South-east or east winds, though disagreeable, cause a violent agitation of the pieces of ice, and so annoy the whales as to induce them to leave their retreat and appear in the open sea. Although the fishery requires a cloudy atmosphere, yet it must be free from fog or continued snow; smooth water, with a breeze of wind, and navigably open, or perfectly solid ice.

The boats and principal instruments employed in the capture of the whale next claim a description. Whale-boats are, of course, peculiarly adapted for the occupation they are intended to be employed in. A well-constructed Greenland boat possesses the following properties:—It floats lightly and safely on the water, is capable of being rowed with great speed, and readily turned round; it is of such capacity, that it carries six or seven men, seven or eight hundred weight of whale-line, and various other materials, and yet retains the necessary properties of safety, buoyancy, and speed, either in smooth water, or where it is exposed to a considerable sea. Whale-boats, being very liable to receive damage, both from whales and ice, are always carver-built—a structure which is easily repaired. They are usually of the following dimensions. Those called six-oared boats, adapted for carrying seven men, six of whom, including the harpooner, are rowers, are generally twenty-six to twenty-eight feet in length, and about five feet nine inches in breadth. Six-men boats, that is, with five rowers and a steersman, are usually twenty-five to twenty-six feet in length, and about five feet three inches in breadth; and four-oared boats are usually twenty-three to twenty-four feet in length, and about five feet, three inches in breadth. The main breadth of the two first classes of boats is at about three-sevenths of the length of the boat, reckoned from the stern; but in the last class it is necessary to have the main breadth within one-third of the length of the boat from the stern. The object of this is to enable the smaller boat to support, without being dragged under water, as great a strain on the lines as those of a larger class; otherwise, if such a boat were sent out by itself, its lines would be always liable to be lost before any assistance could reach it.

The five-oared or six-men boat is that which is in general use; though each fishing-ship generally carries one or two of the largest class. These boats are now commonly built of fir boards, one-half or three-fourths of an inch thick, with timbers, keel, gunwales, stern, and stern-post of oak. An improvement in the timbering of whale-boats has lately been made, by sawing the timber out of very straight grained oak, and bending them to the required form after being made supple by the application of steam, or immersion in boiling water. This improvement, which renders the timbers more elastic than when they are sawn out of crooked oak, and at the same time makes the boat stronger and lighter, was suggested by Thomas Brodrick, esq., of Whitby, ship-builder. Though the principle has long been acted upon in clincher-built boats, with ash timbers, the application to carver-built whale-boats is, I believe, new. The bow and stern of Greenland boats are both sharp, and in appearance very similar, but the stern forms a more acute angle than the bow. The keel has some depression in the middle from which the facility of turning is acquired.

The instruments of general use in the capture of the whale are the harpoon and the lance. The harpoon is an instrument of iron, of about three feet in length. It consists of three conjoined parts, called the "socket," "shank," and "mouth," the latter of which includes the barbs or "withers." This instrument, if we except a small addition to the barbs and some enlargement of dimensions, maintains the same form in which it was originally used in the fishery two centuries ago. At that time, the mouth or barbed extremity was of a triangular shape, united at the shank in the middle of one of the sides, and this being scooped out on each side of the shank formed two simple flat barbs. In the course of last century, an improvement was made by adding another small barb, resembling the beard of a fishhook, within each of the former withers in a reverse position. The two principal withers in the present improved harpoon measure about eight inches in length and six in breadth, the shank is eighteen inches to two feet in length, and four-tenths of an inch in diameter, and the socket, which is hollow, swells from the size of the shank to near two inches diameter, and is about six inches in length. Now, when the harpoon is forced by a blow into the fat of the whale, and the line is held tight, the principal withers seize the strong ligamentous fibres of the blubber, and prevent it from being withdrawn; and, in the event of its being pulled out so far as to remain entangled by one wither only, which is frequently the case, then the little reversed barb, or "stop-wither," as it is called, collecting a number of the same reticulated sinewy fibres, which are very numerous near the skin, prevents the harpoon from being shaken out by the ordinary motions of the whale. The point and exterior edges of the barbs of the harpoon are sharpened to a rough edge by means of a file. This part of the harpoon is not formed of steel, as it is frequently represented, but of common soft iron, so that when blunted it can be readily sharpened by a file, or even by scraping it with a knife.

The most important part in the construction of this instrument is the shank. As this part is liable to be forcibly and suddenly extended, twisted, and bent, it requires to be made of the softest and most pliable iron. That kind which is of the most approved tenacity is made of old horse-shoe nails or *stubs*, which are formed into small rods, and two or three of these welded together, so that should a flaw happen to occur in any one of the rods, the strength of the whole might still be depended on. Some manufacturers inclose a quantity of stub-iron in a cylinder of best foreign iron, and form the shank of the harpoon out of a single rod. A test, sometimes used for trying the sufficiency of a harpoon, is to wind its shank round a bolt of inch-iron, in the form of a close spiral, then to unwind it again, and put it into a straight form. It bears this without injury in the cold state, it is considered as excellent. The breaking of a harpoon is of no less importance than the value of a whale, which is sometimes estimated at more than £1000 sterling. This consideration has induced many ingenious persons to turn their attention towards improving the construction and security of this instrument, but though various alterations have been suggested, such as forming the shank of wire, adding one or two lateral barbs, etc., etc., they have all given place to the simplicity of the ancient harpoon.

Next in importance to the harpoon is the lance, which is a spear of iron of the length of six feet. It consists of a hollow socket, six inches long, swelling from half an inch, the size of the shank, to near two inches in diameter, into which is fitted a four feet stock or handle of fir; a shank, five feet long and half an inch in diameter; and a mouth of steel, which is made very thin, and exceedingly sharp, seven or eight inches in length, and two or two and a half in breadth. Besides these instruments, there is also the harpoon gun. It was invented in the year 1731, and used by some individuals with success. Being however difficult, and somewhat dangerous in its application, it was laid aside for many years. In 1771 or 1772, a new one was produced to the Society of Arts, and received as an original invention. Between 1772 and 1792, the Society expended large sums in premiums to whale-fishers and to artisans for improvements in the gun and harpoon. Since 1792, they have generally been in the habit of offering a premium of ten guineas to the harpooner who should shoot the greatest number of whales in one season, not being less than three. This premium, however, though it has been frequently offered, has been seldom claimed. In its present improved form, as made by Mr. Wallis, gunsmith, Hull, the harpoon-gun consists of a kind of swivel, having a barrel of wrought-iron 24 or 26 inches in length, of 3 inches exterior diameter, and $1\frac{7}{8}$ inches bore. It is furnished with two locks, which act simultaneously, for the purpose of diminishing the liability of the gun missing fire. The shank of the harpoon is double, terminating in a cylindrical knob, fitting the bore of the gun. Between the two parts of the shank is a wire ring, to which is attached the line. Now, when the harpoon is introduced into the barrel of the gun, the ring with the attached line remains on the outside near the mouth of the harpoon, but the instant that it is fired, the ring flies back against the cylindrical knob. The harpoon-gun has been rendered capable of throwing a harpoon near forty yards with effect, yet, on account of the difficulty in the management of it, it has not been very generally adopted.

In the course of the outward passage, the different utensils are fitted for immediate use. One preparation is that which is known by the name of "spanning harpoons." A piece of rope, of the best hemp, called a "fore-ganger," about two and a quarter inches in circumference, and eight or nine yards in length, is spliced closely round the shank of the harpoon, the swelled socket of which prevents the eye of the *splice* from being drawn off. A stock, or handle, six or seven feet in length, is then fitted into the socket, and fastened in its place through the medium of the fore-ganger. The fastening of the stock is sufficient only for retaining it firm in its situation during the discharge of the weapon, but is liable to be disengaged soon afterwards; on which the harpoon, relieved from the shake and twist of this no longer necessary appendage, maintains its hold with better effect. After the stock drops out, it is seldom lost, but still hangs on the line by means of a loop of cord, fixed openly round it, for the purpose of preventing the stock from floating away. Every harpoon is stamped with the name of the ship to which it belongs; and when prepared for use, a private mark, containing the name of the ship and master, with the date of the year written upon leather, is concealed beneath some rope-yarns, wound round the socket of the instrument, and the same is sometimes introduced also into the fore-ganger. These marks serve to identify the harpoons, when any dispute happens to arise relative to the claims of different ships to the same fish and have sometimes proved of essential service in deciding cases which might otherwise have extended to vexatious litigations.

A harpoon thus prepared, with fore-ganger and stock, is said to be "spanned in." In this state, the point or mouth, being very clean and sharp, is preserved in the same condition by a shield of oiled paper or canvas; and the instrument, with its appendages, laid up in a convenient place, ready for being attached to the whale-line in a boat when wanted.

The principal preparations for commencing the fishery are included in the "fitting of the boats." In this work all the people belonging to the ship are employed. The boats are first cleared of all lumber, and then the whale-lines, each consisting of 120 fathoms of rope, about two and a quarter inches in circumference, are spliced to each other, to the amount of about six to each boat, the united length of which is about 720 fathoms, or 4,320 feet; and the whole carefully and beautifully coiled in compartments in the boat prepared for the purpose. A portion of five or six fathoms of the line first put into the boat, called the "stray-line," is left uncovered by that which follows, and coiled by itself in a small compartment at the stern of the boat: it is furnished with a loop or "eye," for the facility of connecting the lines of one boat with those of another. To the upper end of the line is spliced the fore-ganger of a spanned harpoon, thus connecting the harpoon with all the lines in the boat.

Every boat completely fitted is furnished with two harpoons (one spare,) six or eight lances, and five to seven oars, together with the following instruments and apparatus:—A "jack," or flag, fastened to a pole, intended to be displayed as a signal, whenever a whale is harpooned; a "tail-knife," used for perforating the fins or tail of a dead whale; a "mik," or rest, made of wood, for supporting the stock of the harpoon when ready for instant service; an "axe," for cutting the line when necessary; a "pigging," or small bucket, for bailing the boat or wetting the running lines; a "snatch-block;" a "grapnel;" two "boat-hooks;" a "fid;" a wooden "mallet," and "snow-shovel;" also, a small broom and a "swab," together with spare tholes, grommets, etc. In addition to these, the two six-oared or other swiftest boats are likewise furnished with an apparatus, called a "winch," for heaving the lines into the boat after the fish is either killed or has made his escape; and in some ships they also carry a harpoon-gun, and apparatus for loading. The whole of the articles above enumerated are disposed in convenient places throughout the boat. The axe is always placed within the reach of the harpooner, who, in case of an accident, can cut the line in an instant; the harpoon-gun is fixed by its swivel to the boat's stern; the lances are laid in the sides of the boat, upon the thwarts; the hand-harpoon is placed upon the mik, or rest, with its stock, and on the bow of the boat with its point, and the fore-ganger is clearly coiled beneath it, so that the harpoon can be taken up and discharged in a moment. An oar is used for steering, in preference to a rudder, in consequence of its possessing many advantages: an oar does not retard the velocity of the boat so much as a rudder; it is capable of turning the boat when in a state of rest, and more readily than a rudder when in motion; and it can be used for propelling the boat in narrow places of the ice, where the rowers cannot ply their oars, by the process of sculling, and in calms for approaching a whale without noise, by the same operation.

The crew of a whale-ship are separated into divisions, equal in number to the number of the boats. Each division, consisting of a harpooner, a boat-steerer, and a line-manager, together with three or four rowers, constitutes a boat's crew. The harpooner's principal office is, as his name implies, to strike the whale, also to guide the line, or to kill an entangled whale with his lances. When in pursuit he rows the bow-oar. He has the command of the boat. The boat-steerer ranks next to the harpooner; he guides the course of the boat, watches the motions of the whale pursued, intimates its movements to the harpooner, and stimulates the crew to exertion by encouraging exclamations. The line-manager rows the "after-oar" in the boat, and, conjointly with the boat-steerer, attends to the lines when in the act of running out or coiling in. The remainder of the crew pull the oars. Besides these divisions of the seamen of a whaler into boats' crews, they are classed on the passages, and when no whale-fishing is going on, as in other vessels, into watches.

On fishing-stations, when the weather is such as to render the fishery practicable, the boats are always ready for instant service, suspended from davits, or cranes, by the sides of the ship, and furnished with stores, as before enumerated; two boats at least, the crews of which are always in readiness, can in general be manned and lowered into the water within the space of one minute of time. "Wherever there is a probability of seeing whales, when the weather and situation are such as to present a possibility of capturing them, the "crow's nest" is generally occupied by the master, or some one of the officers, who, commanding from thence an extensive prospect of the surrounding sea, keeps an anxious watch for the appearance of a whale. Assisted by a telescope, he views the operations of any ship which may be in sight at a distance; and occasionally sweeps the horizon with his glass, to extend the limited sphere of vision in which he is able to discriminate a whale with the naked eye to an area vastly greater. The moment that a fish is seen, he gives notice to the "watch upon deck," part of whom leap into a boat, are lowered down, and push off towards the place. If the fish be large, a second boat is immediately dispatched to the support of the other. When the whale again appears, two boats row towards it with their utmost speed, and though they may be disappointed in all their attempts, they generally continue the pursuit until the fish either takes the alarm and escapes, or they are recalled by a signal to the ship. When two or more fishes appear at the same time in different situations, the number of boats sent in pursuit is commonly increased. When the whole of the boats are sent out, the ship is said to have "a loose fall." During fine weather, when there is great probability of finding whales, a boat is generally kept in readiness, manned and afloat, sometimes towed by a rope astern, or, if the ship be still, at a little distance. There are several rules observed in approaching a whale, as precautions, to prevent the animal from taking the alarm. As the whale is dull of hearing, but quick of sight, the boat-steerer always endeavours to get behind it, and, in accomplishing this, he sometimes takes a circuitous route. In calm weather, when guns are not used, the greatest caution is necessary before a whale can be reached; smooth careful rowing is always requisite, and sometimes sculling.

When it is known that a whale seldom abides longer on the surface of the water than two minutes, that it generally remains from five to ten or fifteen minutes under water, that in this interval it sometimes moves through the space of half a mile or more, and that the fisher has very rarely any certain intimation of the place in which it will reappear—the difficulty and address requisite to approach sufficiently near, during its short stay on the surface, to harpoon it, will be readily appreciated. It is, therefore, a primary consideration with the harpooner always to place his boat as near as possible to the spot where he expects the fish to rise; and he considers himself successful in the attempt when the fish "comes up within a start," that is, within the distance of about two hundred yards. A whale moving forward, at a small distance beneath the surface of the sea, leaves a sure indication of its situation in what is called "an eddy," having somewhat the resemblance of "the wake," or track of a ship; and in fine calm weather, its change of position is sometimes pointed out by the birds, many of which closely follow it when at the surface, and hover over it when below, whose keener vision can discern it when it is totally concealed from human eye. By these indications many whales have been taken.

The providence of God is manifested in the tameness and timidity of many of the largest inhabitants of the earth and sea, whereby they fall victims to the prowess of man, and are rendered subservient to his convenience in life. And this was the design of the lower animals in their creation, for God, when he made man, gave him "dominion over the fish of the sea, and over the fowl of the air, and over the cattle, and over all the earth, and over every creeping thing that creepeth upon the earth." The holy psalmist, when considering the power and goodness of God in the creation, exclaimed, "What is man, that thou art mindful of him; and the son of man, that thou visitest him?" And, in contemplation of the glory and honour put upon man by the Almighty, in the power given him over created nature, he adds, "Thou madest him to have dominion over the works of thy hands; thou hast put all things under his feet: ... the fowl of the air, and the fish of the sea, and whatsoever passeth through the paths of the seas. O Lord our Lord, how excellent is thy name in all the earth!" Hence, while we admire the cool and determined intrepidity of those who successfully encounter the huge mysticetus, if we are led to reflect on the source of the power by which the strength of men is rendered effectual for the mighty undertaking, our reflections must lead us to the great First Cause as the only source from whence such power could be derived. If there be peril in the encounter between man and God's most powerful creatures, how much more dangerous must be the struggle between man and the Lord his Maker; and how certain, if it be prolonged, the terrible issue of such a contest! The power of the mighty monster of the deep, or even of the most glorious archangel, is as nothing in comparison with Him to whom power belongeth, and who will overwhelm his adversaries with a fearful and final perdition. Now, however, there is no fury in him, and he is as condescending as he is powerful, entreating his rebellious subjects to receive the peace of his reconciliation, and to draw near to him with a penitent and contrite heart, through the merit and intercession of his Son, in whom he assures us of a free and complete forgiveness.

Whenever a whale lies on the surface of the water, unconscious of the approach of its enemies, the hardy fisher rows directly upon it; and, an instant before the boat touches it, buries his harpoon in its back; but if, while the boat is at a little distance, the whale should indicate its intention of diving, by lifting its head above its common level, and then plunging it under water, and raising its body till it appears like a large segment of a sphere, the harpoon is thrown from the hand, or fired from a gun, the former of which methods, when skilfully practised, is efficient at the distance of eight or ten yards, and the latter at the distance of thirty yards, or upward. The wounded whale, in the surprise and agony of the moment, makes a convulsive effort to escape. Then is the moment of danger. The boat is subjected to the most violent blows from its head or its fins, but particularly from its ponderous tail, which sometimes sweeps the air with such tremendous fury, that both boat and men are exposed to one common destruction.

The head of the whale is avoided, because it cannot be penetrated with the harpoon; but any part of the body between the head and the tail will admit of the full length of the instrument, without danger of obstruction. The moment that the wounded whale disappears, or leaves the boat, a jack or flag, elevated on a staff, is displayed, on sight of which those on watch in the ship give the alarm, by stamping on the deck, accompanied by a simultaneous and continuous shout of "a fall." This word, derived from the Dutch language, is expressive of the conduct of the sailors in jumping, dropping, falling to man the boats on an occasion requiring extreme dispatch. At this sound, the sleeping crew arouse, jump from their beds, rush upon deck, with their clothes tied by a string in their hands, and crowd into the boats. With a temperature of zero, should a "fall" occur, the crew would appear on deck, shielded only by their drawers, stockings, and shirts, or other habiliments in which they sleep. They generally contrive to dress themselves in part, at least, as the boats are lowered down, but sometimes they push off in the state in which they rise from their beds, row away towards the "fast-boat," and have no opportunity of clothing themselves for a length of time afterwards. The alarm of "a fall" has a singular effect on the feelings of a sleeping person unaccustomed to the whale-fishing business. It has often been mistaken as a cry of distress. A landsman in a Hull ship, seeing the crew on an occasion of a fall rush upon deck, with their clothes in their hands, and leap into the boats, when there was no appearance of danger, thought the men were all mad; but with another individual the effect was totally different. Alarmed with the extraordinary noise, and still more so when he reached the deck with the appearance of all the crew seated in the boats in their shirts, he imagined the ship was sinking. He therefore endeavoured to get into a boat himself; but every one of them being fully manned, he was always repulsed. After several fruitless endeavours to gain a place among his comrades, he cried out, with feelings of evident distress, "What shall I do?—will none of you take me in?"

The first effort of a "fast-fish," or whale that has been struck, is to escape from the boat by sinking under water. After this, it pursues its course directly downward, or reappears at a little distance, and swims with great celerity near the surface of the water towards any neighbouring ice among which it may obtain an imaginary shelter; or it returns instantly to the surface, and gives evidence of its agony by the most convulsive throes, in which its fins and tail are alternately displayed in the air and dashed into the water with tremendous violence. The former behaviour, however, that is, to dive towards the bottom of the sea, is so frequent in comparison of any other, that it may be considered as the general conduct of a "fast-fish." A whale, struck near the edge of any large sheet of ice, and passing underneath it, will sometimes run the whole of the line out of one boat in the space of eight or ten minutes of time. To retard, therefore, as much as possible, the flight of the whale, and to secure the lines, it is usual for the harpooner to cast one, two, or more turns of the line round a kind of post, called a *bollard*, which is fixed within ten or twelve inches of the stern of the boat for the purpose. Such is the friction of the line, when running round the bollard, that it frequently envelopes the harpooner in smoke; and if the wood were not repeatedly wetted, would probably set fire to the boat.

During the capture of one whale, a groove is sometimes cut in the bollard, near an inch in depth, and were it not for a plate of brass, iron, or a block of lignum vitæ, which covers the top of the stern, where the line passes over, it is apprehended that the action of the line on the material of the boat would cut it down to the water's edge in the course of one season of successful fishing. The approaching distress of a boat for want of line is indicated by the elevation of an oar in the way of a mast, to which is added a second, a third, or even a fourth, in proportion to the nature of the exigence. The utmost care and attention are requisite on the part of every person in the boat when the lines are running out, fatal consequences having been sometimes produced by the most trifling neglect. On my first voyage to the whale-fishery, such an accident occurred. A thousand fathoms of line were already out, and the fast-boat was forcibly pressed against the side of a piece of ice. The harpooner, in his anxiety to retard the flight of the whale, applied too many turns of the line round the bollard, which, getting entangled, drew the boat beneath the ice. Another boat providentially was at hand, into which the crew, including myself, who happened to be present, had just time to escape. The whale, with near two miles length of line, was, in consequence of the accident, lost.

When fish have been struck by myself, I have, on different occasions, estimated their rate of descent. For the first 300 fathoms, the average velocity was usually after the rate of eight to ten miles per hour. In one instance, the third line of 120 fathoms was run out in sixty-one seconds, that is, at the rate of 8·16 miles, or 7·18 nautical miles, per hour. The average stay under water of a wounded whale, which steadily descends after being struck, according to the most usual conduct of the animal, is about thirty minutes. The longest stay I ever observed was fifty-six minutes; but in shallow water I have been informed it has sometimes been known to remain an hour and a half at the bottom after being struck, and yet has returned to the surface alive. The greater the velocity, the more considerable the distance to which it descends, and the longer the time it remains under water, so much greater in proportion is the extent of exhaustion, and the consequent facility of accomplishing its capture. Immediately that it reappears, the assisting boats make for the place with their utmost speed, and as they reach it, each harpooner plunges his harpoon into its back, to the amount of three, four, or more, according to the size of the whale and the nature of the situation. Most frequently, however, it descends for a few minutes after receiving the second harpoon, and obliges the other boats to await its return to the surface before any attack can be made. It is afterwards actively plied with lances, which are thrust into its body, aiming at its vitals. At length, when exhausted by numerous wounds and the loss of blood, which flows from the huge animal in copious streams, it indicates the approach of its dissolution by discharging from its "blow-holes" a mixture of blood along with the air and mucus which it usually expires, and finally jets of blood. The sea to a great extent around is dyed with its blood, and the ice-boats and men are sometimes drenched with the same. Its track is likewise marked by a broad pellicle of oil, which exudes from his wounds, and appears on the surface of the sea. Its final capture is sometimes preceded by a convulsive and energetic struggle, in which its tail, reared, whirled, and violently jerked in the air, resounds to the distance of miles. In dying, it turns on its back, or on its side, which joyful circumstance is announced by the capturers with the striking of their flags, accompanied with three lively huzzas.

The remarkable exhaustion observed on the first appearance of a wounded whale at the surface, after a descent of 700 or 800 fathoms perpendicular, does not depend on the nature of the wound it has received, for a hundred superficial wounds received from harpoons could not have the effect of a single lance penetrating the vitals, but is the effect of the almost incredible pressure to which the animal must have been exposed. The surface of the body of a large whale may be considered as comprising an area of 1,540 square feet. This, under the common weight of the atmosphere alone, must sustain a pressure of 3,104,640 lbs., or 1,386 tons. But at the depth of 800 fathoms, where there is a column of water equal in weight to about 154 atmospheres, the pressure on the animal must be equal to 211,200 tons. This is a degree of pressure of which we can have but an imperfect conception. It may assist our comprehension, however, to be informed, that it exceeds in weight sixty of the largest ships of the British navy, when manned, provisioned, and fitted for a six months' cruise.

By the motions of the fast-boat, the movements of the whale are estimated. Every fast-boat carries a flag, and the ship to which such boats belong also wears a flag, until the whale is either killed or makes its escape. These signals serve to indicate to surrounding ships the exclusive title of the fast-ship to the entangled whale, and to prevent their interference, excepting in the way of assistance in the capture.

With respect to the length of time requisite for capturing a whale, it may be remarked that this greatly depends on the activity of the harpooners, the favourableness of situation and weather, and on the peculiar conduct of the whale attacked. I have myself witnessed the capture of a large whale in twenty-eight minutes, and have also been engaged with another fish, which was lost, after it had been entangled about sixteen hours. Under the most favourable circumstances, the average length of time occupied in the capture of a whale may be stated as not exceeding an hour, and the general average, including all sizes of fish and all circumstances of capture, may probably be two or three hours. The mode described in the preceding pages of conducting the fishery for whales under favourable circumstances, may be considered as the general plan pursued by the fishers of all ports of Britain, as well as of those of other nations who resort to Spitzbergen.

The ease with which some whales are subdued, and the slightness of the entanglement by which they are taken, are truly surprising; but, with others, it is equally astonishing, that neither line nor harpoon, nor any number of each, is sufficiently strong to effect their capture. Whales have even been taken in consequence of the entanglement of a line, without any harpoon at all; though, when such a case has occurred, it has evidently been the result of accident. A harpooner belonging to the Prince of Brazils, of Hull, had struck a small fish. It descended, and remained for some time quiet, and at length appeared to be drowned. The strain on the line being then considerable, it was taken to the ship's capstern, with a view of heaving the fish up. The force requisite for performing this operation was extremely various; sometimes the line came in with ease, at others, a quantity was withdrawn with great force and rapidity. As such, it appeared evident that the fish was yet alive. The heaving, however, was persisted in, and after the greater part of the lines had been drawn on board, a dead fish appeared at the surface, secured by several turns of the line round its body. It was disentangled with difficulty, and was confidently believed to be the whale that had been struck. But when the line was cleared from the fish, it proved to be merely the "bight," for the end still hung perpendicularly downward. What was then the surprise to find that it was still pulled away with considerable force! The capstern was again resorted to, and shortly afterwards they hove up, also dead, the fish originally struck, with the harpoon still fast. Hence, it appeared that the fish first drawn up had got accidentally entangled with the line, and, in its struggles to escape, had still further involved itself, by winding the line repeatedly round its body. The fish first entangled, as was suspected, had long been dead, but it was this interloper that occasioned the jerks and other singular effects observed on the line.

The method already described is that which is adopted for the capture of whales under the most favourable circumstances, and is subject to many alterations when the situation or circumstances are peculiar. Hence arise various modes of capturing the whale, which furnish abundant opportunities for the exercise of ingenuity and skill, and are attended by their peculiar dangers. To an enumeration of these various methods, according to local circumstances, we now proceed to direct the reader's attention.

1. *Pack-fishing.*—The borders of close packs of drift-ice are frequently a favourite resort of large whales. To attack them in such a situation subjects the fisher to great risks in his lines and boats, as well as uncertainty in effecting their capture. When a considerable swell prevails on the borders

of the ice, the whales, on being struck, will sometimes recede from the pack, and become the prize of their assailers; but most generally they flee to it for shelter, and frequently make their escape. To guard against the loss of lines as much as possible, it is usual either to strike two harpoons from different boats at the same moment, or to bridle the lines of a second boat upon those of the boat from which the fish is struck. This operation consists in fixing other lines to those of the fast-boat, at some distance from the harpoon, so that there is only one harpoon and one line immediately attached to the fish, but the double strength of a line from the place of their junction to the boats. Hence, should the fish flee directly into the ice, and proceed to an inaccessible distance, the two boats bearing an equal strain on each of their lines can at pleasure draw the harpoon, or break the single part of the line immediately connected with it, and in either case secure themselves against any considerable loss.

When a pack, from its closeness, prevents boats from penetrating, the men travel over the ice, leaping from piece to piece, in pursuit of the entangled whale. In this pursuit they carry lances with them, and sometimes harpoons, with which, whenever they can approach the fish, they attack it; and if they succeed in killing it, they drag it towards the exterior margin of the ice, by means of the line fastened to the harpoon with which it was originally struck. In such cases, it is generally an object of importance to sink it beneath the ice; for effecting which purpose, each lobe of the tail is divided from the body, excepting a small portion of the edge, from which it hangs pendulous in the water. If it still floats, bags of sand, kedges, or small cannon, are suspended by a block on the bight of the line, wherewith the buoyancy of the dead whale is usually overcome. It then sinks, and is easily hauled out by the line into the open sea.

To particularize all the variety of pack-fishing, arising from wind and weather, size of the fish, state and peculiarities of the ice, etc., would require more space than the interest of the subject to general readers would justify. I shall therefore only remark, that pack-fishing is, on the whole, the most troublesome and dangerous of all others; that instances have occurred of fish having been entangled during forty or fifty hours, and escaped after all; and that other instances are remembered, of ships having lost the greater part of their stock of lines, several of their boats, and sometimes, though happily less commonly, some individuals of their crews.

2. *Field-fishing.* — The fishery for whales, when conducted at the margin of those wonderful sheets of solid ice, called fields, is, when the weather is

fine, and the refuge for ships secure, the most agreeable, and sometimes the most productive of all situations which the fishery of Greenland presents. A fish struck at the margin of a large field of ice generally descends obliquely beneath it, takes four or eight lines from the fast-boat, and then returns exhausted to the edge. It is then attacked in the usual way with harpoons and lances, and is easily killed. There is one evident advantage in field-fishing, which is this: when the fast-boat lies at the edge of a firm unbroken field, and the line proceeds in an angle beneath the ice, the fish must necessarily arise somewhere in a semicircle described from the fast-boat as a centre, with a sweep not exceeding the length of the lines out; but most generally it appears in a line extending along the margin of the ice, so that the boats, when dispersed along the edge of the field, are as effectual and as ready for promoting the capture as twice the number of boats or more when fishing in open situations; because, in open situations, the whale may arise anywhere within a circle, instead of a semicircle, described by the length of the lines withdrawn from the fast-boat, whence it frequently happens that all the attendant boats are disposed in a wrong direction, and the fish recovers its breath, breaks loose, and escapes before any of them can secure it with a second harpoon. Hence, when a ship fishes at a field with an ordinary crew and six or seven boats, two of the largest fish may be struck at the same time with every prospect of success; while the same force attempting the capture of two at once in an open situation, will not unfrequently occasion the loss of both. There have, indeed, been many instances of a ship's crew, with seven boats, striking at a field six fish at the same time, and succeeding in killing the whole; generally speaking, six boats at a field are capable of performing the same execution as near twice that number in open situations. Besides, fields sometimes afford an opportunity of fishing, when in any other situation there can be little or no probability of success, or, indeed, when to fish elsewhere is utterly impracticable. Thus, calms, storms, and fogs, are great annoyances in the fishery in general, and frequently prevent it altogether, but at fields the fishery goes on under any of these disadvantages. As there are several important advantages attending the fishery at fields, so likewise there are some serious disadvantages, chiefly relating to the safety of the ships engaged in the occupation. The motions of fields are rapid, various, and unaccountable, and the power with which they approach each other, and squeeze every resisting object, immense; hence occasionally vast mischief is produced, which it is not always in the power of the most skilful and attentive master to foresee or prevent.

Such are the principal advantages and disadvantages of fields of ice to the whale-fishery. The advantages, however, as above enumerated, though they extend to large floes, do not extend to small floes, or to such fields, how large soever they may be, as contain cracks or holes, or are filled up with thin ice in the interior. Large and firm fields are the most convenient, and likewise the most advantageous for the fishery; the most convenient, because the whales, unable to breathe beneath a close extensive field of ice, are obliged to make their appearance again above water among the boats on the look out; and they are the most advantageous, because not only the most fish commonly resort to them, but a greater number can be killed with less force, and in a shorter space of time, than in any other situation. Thin fields, or fields full of holes, being by no means advantageous to fish by, are usually avoided, because a "fast fish" retreating under such a field, can respire through the holes in the centre as conveniently as on the exterior; and a large fish usually proceeds from one hole to another, and if determined to advance, cannot possibly be stopped. In this case, all that can be done is, to break the line or draw the harpoon out. But when the fish can be observed blowing in any of the holes in a field, the men travel over the ice, and attack it with lances, pricking it over the nose to endeavour to turn it back. This scheme, however, does not always answer the expectations of the fishers, as frequently the fear of his enemies acts so powerfully on the whale that he pushes forward towards the interior to his dying moment. When killed, the same means are used as in pack-fishing to sink it, but they do not always succeed; for the harpoon is frequently drawn out, or the line broken in the effort. If, therefore, no attempt to sink the fish avails, there is scarcely any other practicable method of making a prize of it, (unless when the ice happens to be so thin that it can be broken with a boat, or a channel readily cut in it with an ice-saw,) than cutting the blubber away, and dragging it piece by piece across the ice to the vessel, which requires immense labour, and is attended with vast loss of time. Hence we have a sufficient reason for avoiding such situations, whenever fish can be found elsewhere.

As connected with this subject, I cannot pass over a circumstance which occurred within my own observation, and which excited my highest admiration. On the 8th July, 1813, the ship Esk lay by the edge of a thin sheet of ice, in which were several thin parts and some holes. Here a fish being heard blowing, a harpoon, having a line connected with it, was conveyed across the ice by a boat on guard, and the harpooner succeeded in striking the whale, at the distance of 350 yards from the verge. It dragged out ten lines, (2,400 yards,) and was supposed to be seen blowing in different holes in the ice. After some time, it happened to make its appearance on the exterior, when a harpoon was struck at the moment it was on the point of proceeding again beneath. About a hundred yards from the edge, it broke the ice where it was a foot in thickness with its crown, and respired through the opening. It then determinately pushed forward, breaking the ice as it advanced, in spite of the lances continually directed against it. It reached at length a kind of basin in the field, where it floated on the surface of the water without any encumbrance from ice. Its back being fairly exposed, the harpoon struck from the boat was observed to be so slightly entangled that it was ready to drop out. Some of the officers lamented this circumstance, and expressed a wish that the harpoon were better fast, observing at the same time that if it should slip out, the fish would either be lost, or they would be under the necessity of flensing it where it lay, and of dragging the pieces of blubber over the ice to the ship, a kind and degree of labour every one was anxious to avoid. No sooner was the wish expressed, and its importance made known, than one of the sailors, a smart and enterprising fellow, stepped forward and volunteered his services to strike it better in. Not at all intimidated by the surprise which was manifested in every countenance by such a bold proposal, he pulled out his pocket-knife, leapt upon the back of the living whale, and immediately cut the harpoon out. Stimulated by this courageous example, two of his companions proceeded to his assistance. While one of them hauled upon the line, and held it in his hands, the other set his shoulder against the extremity of the harpoon, and, though it was without a stock, he contrived to strike it again into the fish more effectually than it was at first. The fish was in motion before this was finished. After they got off its back, it advanced a considerable distance, breaking the ice all the way, and survived this uncommon treatment ten or fifteen minutes. This admirable act was an essential benefit. The fish sunk spontaneously after being killed, on which it was hauled out to the edge of the ice by the line, and secured without further trouble. It proved a stout whale, and a very acceptable prize.

When a ship approaches a considerable field of ice, and finds whales, it is usual to moor to the leeward side of it, from which the adjoining ice generally first separates. Boats are then placed on watch on each side of the ship, and stationed at intervals of one hundred or one hundred and fifty yards along the edge of the ice. Hence, if a fish arises anywhere between the extreme boats, it seldom escapes unhurt. It is not uncommon for a great number of ships to moor to the same sheet of ice. When the whale-fishery of the Hollanders was in a flourishing state, above one hundred sail of ships might sometimes be seen moored to the same field of ice, each having two or more boats on watch. The field would in consequence, be so nearly surrounded with boats, that it was almost impossible for a fish to rise near the verge of the ice without being within the limits of a start of some of them.

3. *Fishing in crowded ice or in open packs.* —In navigable open drift-ice, or amongst small detached streams and patches, either of which serve in a degree to break the force of the sea, and to prevent any considerable swell from arising, we have a situation which is considered as one of the best possible for conducting the fishery in; consequently, it comes under the same denomination as those favourable situations in which I have first attempted to describe the proceedings of the fishers in killing the whale. But the situation I now mean to refer to is when the ice is crowded and nearly close, so close, indeed, that it scarcely affords room for boats to pass through it, and by no means sufficient space for a ship to be navigated among it. This kind of situation occurs in somewhat open packs, or in large patches of crowded ice, and affords a fair probability of capturing a whale, though it is seldom accomplished without a considerable deal of trouble. When the ice is very crowded, and the ship cannot sail into it with propriety, it is usual, especially with foreigners, to seek out for a mooring to some mass of ice, if such can be found, extending two or three fathoms or more under water. A piece of ice of this kind is capable not only of holding the ship "head to wind," but also to windward of the smaller ice. The boats then set out in chase of any fish which may be seen, and when one happens to be struck, they proceed in the capture in a similar manner as when under more favourable circumstances, excepting so far as the obstruction which the quality and arrangement of the ice may offer to the regular system of proceeding. Among crowded ice, for instance, the precise direction pursued by the fish is not easily ascertained, nor can the fish itself be readily discovered on its first arrival at the surface after being struck, on account of the elevation of the intervening masses of ice, and the great quantity of line it frequently takes from the fast-boat. Success in such a situation depends on the boats being spread widely abroad, and on a judicious arrangement of each boat; on a keen look out on the part of the harpooners in the boats, and on their occasionally taking the benefit of a hummock of ice, from the elevation of which the fish may sometimes be seen blowing in the interstices of the

ice; on pushing or rowing the boats with the greatest imaginable celerity towards the place where the fish may have been seen; and lastly, on the exercise of the highest degree of activity and dispatch in every proceeding.

If these be neglected, the fish will generally have taken breath, recovered its strength, and removed to some other quarter, before the arrival of the boats; and it is often remarked, that if there be one part of the ice more crowded or more difficult of access than another, it commonly retreats thither for refuge. In such cases, the sailors find much difficulty in getting to it with their boats, having to separate many pieces of ice before they can pass through between them. But when it is not practicable to move the pieces, and when they cannot travel over them, they must either drag the boats across the intermediate ice, or perform an extensive circuit before they can reach the opposite side of the close ice, into which the whale has retreated.

A second harpoon in this case, as indeed in all others, is a material point. They proceed to lance whenever the second harpoon is struck, and strike more harpoons as the auxiliary boats progressively arrive at the place. When the fish is killed, it is often at a distance from the ship, and so circumstanced that the ship cannot get near it. In such cases, the fish must be towed by the boats to the ship; an operation which, among crowded ice, is most troublesome and laborious.

4. *Bay-ice fishing.*—Bay-ice constitutes a situation which, though not particularly dangerous, is yet, on the whole, one of the most troublesome in which whales are killed. In sheets of bay-ice, the whales find a very effectual shelter; for so long as the ice will not carry a man, they cannot be approached with a boat without producing such a noise as must certainly warn them of the intended assault; and if a whale, by some favourable accident, were struck, the difficulties of completing the capture are always numerous, and sometimes prove insurmountable. The whale having free locomotion beneath the ice, the fishers pursue it under great disadvantage. The fishers cannot push their boats toward it but with extreme difficulty, while the whale, invariably warned by the noise of their approach, possesses every facility for avoiding its enemies.

In the year 1813, I adopted a new plan of fishing in bay-ice, which was attended with the most successful result. The ship under my command, the Esk, of Whitby, was frozen into a sheet of bay-ice, included in a triangular space, formed by several massive fields and floes. Here a number of small whales were seen sporting around us in every little hole or space in the bay-ice, and occasionally they were observed to break through it for the purpose of breathing. In various little openings free of ice near the ship, few of which were twenty yards in diameter, we placed boats, each equipped with a harpoon and lines, and directed by two or three men. They had orders to place themselves in such a situation that if a fish appeared in the same opening they could scarcely fail of striking it. Previous to this, I supplied myself with a pair of ice-shoes, consisting of two pieces of thin deal, six feet in length, and seven inches in breadth. They were made very thin at both ends, and in the centre of each was a hollow place, exactly adapted for the reception of the sole of my boot, with a loop of leather for confining the toes. I was thus enabled to retain the ice-shoes pretty firmly to my feet when required, or, when I wished it, to disengage them in a moment. Where the ice was smooth, it was easy to move in a straight line, but in turning I found a considerable difficulty, and required some practice before I could effect it without falling. I advanced with tolerable speed, where the ice was level on the surface, by sliding the shoes alternately forward, but when I met with rough hilly places I experienced great inconvenience. When, however, the rough places happened to consist of strong ice, which generally was the case, I stept out of my ice-shoes until I reached a weaker part. Equipped with this apparatus, I travelled safely over ice which had not been frozen above twenty-four hours, and which was incapable of supporting the weight of the smallest boy in the ship.

Whenever a fish was struck, I gave orders to the harpooner, in running the line, to use every means of drowning it; the trouble of hauling it up, under the circumstances in which the ship was placed, being a matter of no consideration. This was attempted by holding a steady tight strain on the line, without slacking it or jerking it unnecessarily, and by forbearing to haul the line when the fish stopped. By this measure, one fish, the stoutest of the three which we got, was drowned. When others were struck, and the attempt to drown them failed, I provided myself with a harpoon, and observing the direction of the line, travelled towards the place where I expected the fish to rise. A small boat was launched, more leisurely, in the same direction for my support; and whenever the ice in my track was capable of supporting a man, assistance was afforded me in dragging the line. When the wounded fish appeared, I struck my harpoon through the ice, and then, with some occasional assistance, proceeded to lance it, until it was killed. At different times, the fish rose beneath my feet, and broke the ice on which I stood; on one occasion, where the ice was happily more than usually strong, I was obliged to leave my ice shoes, and skip off. In this way we captured three fish, and took their produce on board, while several ships near us made not the least progress in the fishery. After they were killed, we had much trouble in getting them to the ship, but as we could not employ ourselves to advantage in any other way, we were well satisfied with the issue. This part of the business I could not effect alone, and all hands, who were occasionally employed in it, broke through the ice. Some individuals broke in two or three times, but no serious accident ensued. As a precaution, we extended a rope from man to man, which was held in the hands of each in their progress across the ice, and which served for drawing those out of the water who happened to break through. Sometimes ten or a dozen of them would break in at once, but so far was such an occurrence from exciting distress, that each of their companions indulged a laugh at their expense, notwithstanding they probably shared the same fate a minute or two afterwards.

5. *Fishing in storms.*—Excepting in situations sheltered from the ice, it would be alike useless and presumptuous to attempt to kill whales during a storm. Instances, however, occur, wherein fish that were struck during fine weather, or in winds which do not prevent the boats from plying about, remain entangled, but unsubdued, after the commencement of a storm. Sometimes the capture is completed, at others the fishers are under the necessity of cutting the lines, and allowing the whale to escape. Sometimes, when they have succeeded in killing it, and in securing it during the gale with a hawser to the ship, they are enabled to make a prize of it on the return of moderate weather; at others, after having it to appearance secured by means of a sufficient rope, the dangerous proximity of an ice-pack constrains them to cut it adrift and abandon it for the preservation of their vessel. After thus being abandoned, it becomes the prize of the first who gets possession of it, though it be in the face of the original capturers. A storm commencing while the boats are engaged with an entangled fish, sometimes occasions serious disasters. Generally, however, though they suffer the loss of the fish, and perhaps some of their boats and materials, yet the men escape with their lives.

6. *Fishing in foggy weather.*—The fishery in storms can never be voluntary; but in foggy weather, though occasionally attended with hazard, the fishery is not altogether impracticable. The fogs which occur in the icy regions in June and July are generally dense and lasting: they are so thick, that objects cannot be distinguished at the distance of 100 or 150 yards, and frequently

continue for several days without attenuation. To fish with safety and success, during a thick fog, is, therefore, a matter of difficulty, and of still greater uncertainty. When it happens that a fish conducts itself favourably, that is, descends almost perpendicularly, and, on its return to the surface, remains nearly stationary, or moves round in a small circle, the capture is usually accomplished without hazard or particular difficulty; but when, on the contrary, it proceeds with any considerable velocity in a horizontal direction, or obliquely downwards, it soon drags the boats out of sight of the ship, and shortly so confounds the fishers in the intensity of the mist, that they lose all traces of the situation of their vessel. If the fish, in its flight, draws them beyond the reach of the sound of a bell, or a horn, their personal safety becomes endangered; and if they are removed beyond the sound of cannon, their situation becomes extremely hazardous, especially if no other ships happen to be in the immediate vicinity. Meanwhile, whatever may be their imaginary or real danger, the mind of their commander must be kept in the most anxious suspense until they are found; and whether they may be in safety or near perishing with fatigue, hunger, and cold, so long as he is uncertain of their fate, his anxiety must be the same.

Before entering on the subsequent operations of the whalers, connected with a successful fishery, I shall give a few examples of remarkable strength, activity, or other peculiarity, in the behaviour of whales after they have been struck, being a few of the curious circumstances connected with the fishery which I have myself observed, or have received from unquestionable authority. On the 25th June, 1812, one of the harpooners belonging to the Resolution, of Whitby, under my command, struck a whale by the edge of a small floe of ice; assistance being promptly afforded, a second boat's lines were attached to those of the fast-boat in a few minutes after the harpoon was discharged; the remainder of the boats proceeded to some distance in the direction which the fish seemed to have taken. In about a quarter of an hour, the fast-boat, to my surprise, again made a signal for lines. As the ship was then within five minutes' sail, we instantly steered towards the boat, with the view of affording assistance by means of a spare boat we still retained on board. Before we reached the place, however, we observed four oars displayed in signal order, which, by their number, indicated a most urgent necessity for assistance. Two or three men were at the same time seen seated close by the stern, which was considerably elevated, for the purpose of keeping it down, while the bow of the boat, by the force of the line, was drawn down to the level of the sea, and the harpooner, by the friction of the line round the bollard, was enveloped in smoky obscurity. At length, when the ship was scarcely one hundred yards distant, we perceived preparations for quitting the boat. The sailors' pea jackets were cast upon the adjoining ice; the oars were thrown down; the crew leaped overboard; the bow of the boat was buried in the water; the stern rose perpendicularly, and then majestically disappeared. The harpooner having caused the end of the line to be fastened to the iron ring at the boat's stern was the means of its loss; and a *tongue* of the ice, on which was a depth of several feet of water, kept the boat, by the pressure of the line against it, at such a considerable distance as prevented the crew from leaping upon the floe. Some of them were, therefore, put to the necessity of swimming for their preservation, but all of them succeeded in scrambling upon the ice, and were taken on board the ship in a few minutes. It may be here observed, that it is an uncommon circumstance for a fish to require more than two boats' lines in such a situation; none of our harpooners, therefore, had any scruple in leaving the fast-boat, never suspecting, after it had received the assistance of one boat with six lines, or upward, that it would need any more.

Several ships being about us, there was a possibility that some person might attack and make a prize of the whale, when it had so far escaped us that we no longer retained any hold of it; as such, we set all sail the ship could safely sustain, and worked through several narrow and intricate channels in the ice in the direction I observed the fish had retreated. After a little time, it was descried by the people in the boats at a considerable distance to the eastward; a general chase immediately commenced, and within the space of an hour three harpoons were struck. We now imagined that the fish was secure, but our expectations were premature. The whale resolutely pushed beneath a large floe that had been recently broken to pieces by the swell, and soon drew all the lines out of the second fast-boat, the officer of which, not being able to get any assistance, tied the end of his line to a hummock of ice and broke it. Soon afterwards, the other two boats, still *fast*, were dragged against the broken floe, when one of the harpoons drew out. The lines of only one boat, therefore remained fast to the fish, and this, with six or eight lines out, was dragged forward into the shattered floe with astonishing force; pieces of ice, each of which were sufficiently large to have answered the purpose of a mooring for the ship, were wheeled about by the strength of the whale; and such was the tension and elasticity of the line that, whenever it slipped clear of any mass of ice, after turning it round into the space between any two adjoining pieces, the boat and its crew flew forward through the crack with the velocity of an arrow, and never failed to launch several feet upon the first mass of ice that it encountered.

While we scoured the sea around the broken floe of the ship, and while the ice was attempted in vain by the boats, the whale continued to press forward in an easterly direction towards the sea. At length, when fourteen lines, about 1,680 fathoms, were drawn from the fourth fast-boat, a slight entanglement of the line broke it at the stern. The fish again made its escape, taking along with it a boat and twenty-eight lines. The united length of the lines was 6,720 yards, or upwards of three English miles and three-quarters; value with the boat above £150 sterling. The obstruction of the sunken boat to the progress of the fish must have been immense, and that of the lines likewise considerable, the weight of the lines alone being thirty-five hundred weight. So long as the fourth fast-boat, through the medium of its lines, retained its hold of the fish, we searched the adjoining sea with the ship in vain, but in a short time after the line was divided we got sight of the object of pursuit at the distance of near two miles to the eastward of the ice and boats, in the open sea. One boat only with lines, and two empty boats, were reserved by the ship. Having, however, happily fine weather and a breeze of wind, we immediately gave chase under all sails, though it must be confessed with the insignificant force by us, the distance of the fish, and the rapidity of its flight considered, we had but very small hopes of success. At length, after pursuing it five or six miles, being at least nine miles from the place where it was struck, we came up with it, and it seemed inclined to rest after its extraordinary exertion. The two dismantled or empty boats having been furnished with two lines each, (a very inadequate supply,) they, together with the one in good state of equipment, now made an attack upon the whale. One of the harpooners made a blunder; the fish saw the boat, took the alarm, and again fled. I now supposed it would be seen no more; nevertheless, we chased nearly a mile in the direction I imagined it had taken, and placed the boats to the best of my judgment in the most advantageous situations. In this instance we were extremely successful. The fish rose near one of the boats, and was immediately harpooned. In a few minutes, two more harpoons entered its back, and lances were plied against it with vigour and success. Exhausted by its amazing exertions to escape, it yielded itself at length to its fate, received the piercing wounds of the lances without resistance, and finally died without a struggle. After all, it may seem surprising that it was not a particularly large individual, the largest lamina of whalebone only measuring nine feet six inches, while those affording twelve feet bone are not uncommon. The quantity of line withdrawn from the different boats engaged in the capture was singularly great. It amounted altogether to 10,440 yards, or nearly six English miles. Of these, thirteen new lines were lost, together with the sunken boat, the harpoon connecting them with the fish having dropped out before the whale was killed. Thus terminated with success an attack upon a whale, which exhibited the most uncommon determination to escape from its pursuers, seconded by the most amazing strength, of any individual whose capture I ever witnessed.

When engaged in the pursuit of a large whale, it is a necessary precaution for two boats at all times to proceed in company, that the one may be able to assist the other on any emergency. With this principle in view, two boats from the Esk were sent out in chase of some large whales, on the 13th of June, 1814. No ice was within sight, the boats had proceeded some time together, when they separated in pursuit of two whales, not far distant from each other, when, by a singular coincidence, the harpooners each struck his fish at the same moment. They were a mile from the ship. Urgent signals for assistance were immediately displayed by each boat, and, in a few minutes, one of the harpooners was under the necessity of slipping the end of his line. Happily, the other fish did not descend so deep, and the lines in the boat proved adequate to the occasion. One of the fish being then supposed to be lost, five of the boats, out of seven, attended on the fish which yet remained entangled, and speedily killed it. A short time afterwards, the other fish supposed to be irrecoverably lost, was descried at a little distance from the place where it was struck; three boats proceeded against it; it was immediately struck, and in twenty minutes also killed. Thus were successfully captured two whales, both of which had been despaired of. They produced us near forty tuns of oil, value at that time £1,400. The lines attached to the fish last killed were recovered in a remarkable manner. The harpooners were busily engaged in attempting to secure them, when the harpoon, by which alone they were prevented from sinking, slipped out; but as it descended in the water, it luckily hooked the line belonging to another boat, by which both harpoon and lines were preserved.

It is very generally believed by the whalers, that fish have occasionally been struck, which, by sudden extension or heave of the body, have instantly disengaged themselves from the harpoon. This usually happens when the whale is struck "with a slack back," as that position of the fish is denominated, in which the back being depressed the flesh is relaxed. A harpoon then struck occasions an uncommon wound. Hence, if the fish suddenly extends itself and elevates its back, the wound appears of twice the size of the harpoon, and consequently the weapon is capable of being thrown out by the jerk of the body. Under such circumstances as these, a large whale was struck by a harpooner belonging to the ship Howe, of Shields. The fish extending and lifting its back with uncommon violence, the harpoon was disengaged and projected high into the air, when, at the same moment, the fish rolled over upon its back, and received the point of the falling weapon in its belly, whereby it was captured and caught. This circumstance, romantic as it may appear, is so well authenticated by the person who struck the fish, together with others who were in the boat at the same time, and were witnesses of the fact, that I have no scruple in introducing it here.

On the 28th of May, 1817, the Royal Bounty, of Leith, captain Drysdale, fell in with a great number of whales, in the lat. 77° 25′ north, and long. 5° or 6° east. Neither ice nor land was in sight, nor was there supposed to be either the one or the other within fifty or sixty miles. A brisk breeze of wind prevailed, and the weather was clear. The boats were, therefore, manned and sent in pursuit. After a chase of about five hours, the harpooner, commanding a boat, who, with another in company, had rowed out of sight of the ship, struck one of the whales. This was about four a.m., of the 29th. The captain, supposing from the long absence of the two most distant boats that a fish had been struck, directed the course of the ship towards the place where he had last seen them, and about eight a.m. he got sight of a boat which displayed the signal for being *fast*. Some time afterwards, he observed the other boat approach the fish, a second harpoon struck, and the usual signal displayed. As, however, the fish dragged the two boats away with considerable speed, it was midday before any assistance could reach them. Two more harpoons were then struck, but such was the vigour of the whale that, although it constantly dragged through the water four to six boats, together with a length of 1,600 fathoms of line which it had drawn out of the different boats, yet it pursued its flight nearly as fast as a boat could row and such was the terror that it manifested on the approach of its enemies, that, whenever a boat passed beyond its tail, it invariably dived. All their endeavours to lance it were, therefore, in vain.

The crews of the loose boats being unable to keep pace with the fish, caught hold of and moored themselves to the fast-boats; and for some hours afterwards, all hands were constrained to sit in idle impatience, waiting for some relaxation in the speed of the whale. Its most general course had hitherto been to windward, but a favourable change taking place, enabled the ship, which had previously been at a great distance, to join the boats at eight p.m. They succeeded in tacking one of the lines to the ship which was fast to the fish, with a view of retarding its flight. They then furled the top-gallant sails, and lowered the top sails; but after supporting the ship a few minutes head to wind, the wither of the harpoon upset or twisted aside, and the instrument was disengaged from its grasp. The whale immediately set off to windward with increased speed, and it required an interval of three hours before the ship could again approach it. Another line was then taken on board, which immediately broke. A fifth harpoon had previously been struck, to replace the one which had been pulled out, but the line attached to it was soon afterwards cut. They then instituted various schemes for arresting the speed of the fish, which occupied their close attention nearly two hours. But its velocity was yet such that the master, who had himself proceeded to the attack, was unable to approach sufficiently near to strike a harpoon. After a long chase, however, he succeeded in getting hold of one of the lines which the fish dragged after it, and in fastening another line to it. The fish then happily turned towards the ship, which was a considerable distance to leeward.

At four p.m. of the 30th, thirty-six hours after the fish had been struck, the ship again joined the boats, when, by a successful manœuvre, they secured two of the fast lines on board. The wind blowing a moderately brisk breeze, the top-gallant sails were taken in, the courses hauled up, and the top sails clewed down, but, notwithstanding the resistance a ship thus situated must necessarily offer, she was towed by the fish directly to windward with the velocity of at least one-half to two knots during an hour and a half; and then, though the whale must have been greatly exhausted, it beat the water with its fins and tail in so tremendous a way, that the sea around was in a continual foam, and the most hardy of the sailors scarcely dared to approach it. At length, about eight p.m., after forty hours of almost incessant, and for the most part fruitless exertion, this formidable and astonishing animal was killed. The capture and the flensing occupied forty-eight hours. The fish was eleven feet four inches in bone, (the length of the longest lamina of whalebone,) and its produce filled forty-seven butts, or twenty-three and a half tun casks, with blubber.

I proceed now to enumerate the proceedings of the fishers after a whale is killed. Some preliminary measures are requisite before a whale can be flensed. The first operation performed on a dead whale is to lash it with a rope, passed several times through two holes pierced through the tail to the bow of the boat. The more difficult operation of freeing the whale from the entanglement of the line is then attempted. As the whale, when dead, always lies on its back or on its side, the lines and harpoons are generally far under water. When they are seen passing obliquely downwards, they are hooked with a grapnel, pulled to the surface, and cut. But, when they hang perpendicular, or when they cannot be seen, they are discovered by a process called "sweeping a fish." This is performed by taking a part of a whale-line in two different boats, ten or fifteen fathoms asunder, and while one boat lies at rest, supporting the end of a line, the other is rowed round the fish, and the bight or intermediate part of the line allowed to sink below the fish as it proceeds, until each of the parts held in the two boats are again brought together. Hence, when one part of the line has made a circuit of the fish, it must evidently inclose every other line or appendage affixed to it. Thus inclosed, they are pulled up to the surface of the water, and each of them cut at the splice of the fore-ganger, leaving the harpoon sticking in the fish, with its fore-ganger attached, and allowing the end of the line to sink, and be hauled on board of the boat from whence it was withdrawn at the convenience of the crew. While this is in progress, the men of other boats, having first lashed the tail to a boat, are employed in lashing the fins together across the belly of the whale.

On one occasion I was myself engaged in the capture of a fish, upon which, when to appearance dead, I leaped, cut holes in the fins, and was in the act of "reeving" a rope through them to lash them together, when the fish sank beneath my feet. As soon as I observed that the water had risen above my knees, I made a spring towards a boat, at the distance of three or four yards from me, and caught hold of the gunwale. Scarcely was I helped on board, before the fish began to move forward, turn from its back upon its belly, reared its tail aloft, and began to shake it with such prodigious violence, as to resound through the air to the distance of two or three miles. In the meanwhile all the sailors very properly kept aloof, and beheld its extraordinary power with the greatest astonishment. After two or three minutes of this violent exercise, it ceased, rolled upon its side, and died.

A fish being properly secured, is then "taken in tow;" that is, all the boats form themselves in a line, by ropes always carried for the purpose, and unite their efforts in rowing towards the ship. Towing a fish is usually considered a cheerful though laborious operation, and is generally performed with great expressions of joy. A large whale, by means of six boats, can be towed at a rate of nearly a mile per hour. The fish having reached the ship, is taken to the larboard side, arranged and secured for flensing. For the performance of this operation, a variety of knives and other instruments are requisite. Towards the stern of the ship the head of the fish is directed, and the tail, which is first cut off, rests abreast of the fore-chains; the smallest or posterior part of the whale's body, where the tail is united, is called the rump, and the extremity or anterior part of the head, the nose or nose-end. The rump, then, supported by a tackle, is drawn forward by means of a stout rope, called the rump-rope; and the head is drawn in an opposite direction, by means of the "nose-tackle." Hence the body of the fish is forcibly extended. The right-side fin, being next the ship, is lashed upwards towards the gunwale. A band of blubber, two or three feet in width, encircling the fish's body, and lying between the fins and the head, being the fat of the neck, or what corresponds in other animals with the neck, is called the kent, because by means of it the fish is turned over, or kented. Now, to the commencement of this imaginary band of fat, or kent, is fixed the lower extremity of a combination of powerful blocks, called the kent-purchase. Its upper extremity is fixed round the head of the main-mast, and its fall or rope is applied to the windlass, drawn tight, and the upper surface of the fish raised several inches above the water. The enormous weight of a whale prevents the possibility of raising it more than one-fourth or one-fifth part out of the water, except indeed when it has been some days dead, in which case it swells, in consequence of air generated by putrefaction, until one-third of its bulk appears above the surface. The fish then lying belly upward, extended, and well secured, is ready for commencing the operation of flensing. In this state a suspension of labour is generally allowed, in which the crew refresh themselves and prepare for the ensuing duties.

An unhappy circumstance once occurred in an interval of this kind. At that period of the fishery, (forty or fifty years ago,) when a single stout whale was sufficient to remunerate the owners of a ship for the expenses of the voyage, great joy was exhibited on the capture of a whale by the fishers. They not only had a dram of spirits, but were sometimes provided with some favourite "mess," on which to regale themselves before they commenced the arduous task of flensing. At such a period, the crew of an English vessel had captured their first whale. It was taken to the ship, placed on the lee-side, and though the wind blew a strong breeze, it was fastened only by a small rope attached to the fin. In this state of supposed security, all hands retired to regale themselves, the captain himself not excepted. The ship being at a distance from any ice, and the fish believed to be secure, they made no great haste in their enjoyment. At length, the specksioneer, having spent sufficient time in indulgence and equipment, with an air of importance and self-confidence, proceeded on deck, and naturally turned to look on the whale. To his astonishment it was not there. In some alarm, he looked astern, ahead, on the other side, but his search was useless; the ship drifting fast had pressed forcibly upon the whale, the rope broke, the fish sank, and was lost. The mortification of this event may be conceived, but the termination of their vexation will not easily be imagined, when it is known that no other opportunity of procuring a whale occurred during the voyage. The ship returned home clean. The blessings of Divine Providence, of a temporal and also of a spiritual kind, are bestowed and continued in union with the activity and watchfulness of those who receive them, and it is a law of the earthly, and also of the heavenly treasure, that "whosoever hath, to him shall be given; and whosoever hath not, from him shall be taken even that which he seemeth to have."

After the whale is properly secured, and the men are sufficiently refreshed, the harpooners, having their feet armed with "spurs," to prevent them from slipping, descend upon the fish. Two boats, each of which is under the guidance of one or two boys, attend upon them, and serve to hold all their knives and other apparatus. Thus provided, the harpooners, directed by the specksioneer, divide the fat into oblong pieces, or "slips," by means of "blubber-spades" and "blubber-knives;" then affixing a "speck-tackle" to each slip, progressively flay it off as it is drawn upward. The speck-tackles, which are two or three in number, are rendered effective by capsterns, winches, or other mechanical powers. Each of them consists of a simple combination of two single blocks, one of which is securely fixed in a strong rope, extended between the main-top and the fore-top, called a guy, and the other is attached by a strap to the blubber of the whale. The flensers commence with the belly and under-jaw, being the only part then above water. The blubber, in pieces of half a ton to a ton each, is received upon deck by the boat-steerers and line-managers, the former with "strand-knives" divide it into portable, cubical, or oblong pieces, containing near a solid foot of fat, while the latter, furnished with "pick-haaks," pass it between decks, down a hole in the main-hatches. It is then received by two men styled kings, who pack it in a receptacle provided for it in the hold, or other suitable place, called the flense-gut, where it remains until further convenience.

All the fat being taken away from the belly, and the right fin removed, the fish is then turned on its side, by means of the kent, which, by the power of the windlass, readily performs this office. The upper surface of fat is again removed, together with the left fin, and after a second kenting one of the "lips" is taken away, by which the whale-bone of one side of the head, now lying nearly horizontal, is exposed. The fish being a little further turned, the whalebone of the left side is dislodged by the use of the "bone hand-spikes," "bone-knives," and "bone-spades." Four instruments, which, when combined, constitute what is called the bone-geer, are used, with the assistance of two speck-tackles, for taking up the whalebone in one mass. On its arrival on deck, it is split with "bone-wedges" and "junks," containing from five to ten blades each, and stowed away. A further kenting brings the fish's back upward, and the next exposes the second side of bone. As the fish is turned or kented round, every part of the blubber becomes progressively uppermost and is removed. At length, when the whole of the blubber, whalebone, and jawbones have been taken on board, the kent, which now appears a slip of perhaps thirty feet in length, is also separated, together with the rump-rope and nose-tackle, on which the carcase being at liberty, generally sinks in the water and disappears. When it floats, however, it becomes food for bears, sharks, and various kinds of birds, all of which attack it with the most voracious earnestness. It is known by the name of the kreng.

When sharks are present, they generally take the liberty of helping themselves very bountifully during the progress of the flensing, but they often pay for their temerity with their lives. Fulmars pay close attendance in immense numbers. They seize the fragments occasionally disengaged by the knife while they are swimming in the water, but most of the other gulls who attend on the occasion take their share on the wing. The burgomaster is decidedly the master of the feast. Hence, every other bird is obliged to relinquish the most delicious morsel when the burgomaster descends to claim it. Bears seldom approach so near the ship as to become partakers of the banquet. When dispatch is seconded by ability, the operation of flensing can be accomplished on a fish affording from twenty to thirty tons of blubber in the space of three or four hours, and, probably, the average time with British fishers but little exceeds four hours.

Some years ago, I was witness of a circumstance in which a harpooner was exposed to the most imminent risk of his life, at the conclusion of a flensing process, by a very curious accident. This harpooner stood on one of the jaw-bones of a fish with a boat by his side. In this situation, while he was in the act of cutting the kreng adrift, a boy inadvertently struck the point of the boat-hook, with which he usually held the boat, through the ring of the harpooner's spur, and in the same act seized the jawbone of the fish with the hook of the same instrument. Before this was discovered, the kreng was set at liberty, and began instantly to sink. The harpooner then threw himself towards the boat, but being firmly entangled by the foot, he fell into the water. Providentially he caught the gunwale of the boat with his hands, but, overpowered by the force of the sinking kreng, he was on the point of relinquishing his grasp when some of his companions got hold of his hands, while others threw a rope round his body. The carcase of the fish was suspended entirely by the poor fellow's body, which was, consequently, so dreadfully extended that there was some danger of his being drawn asunder. But such was his terror of being taken under water, and not, indeed, without cause, for he could never have risen again, that, notwithstanding the excruciating pain he suffered, he constantly cried out to his companions to "haul away the rope." He remained in that dreadful state until means were adopted for hooking the kreng with the grapnel, and bringing it back to the surface of the water. Had he not caught hold of the boat as he was sinking and met with such prompt assistance, he must infallibly have perished.

Next to the process of flensing is that of making-off. When the flens-gut is filled with blubber, or when, no fish being seen, a favourable opportunity of leisure is presented, the operation of making-off is generally commenced. This consists of freeing the fat from all extraneous substances, especially the muscular parts and the skin, then cutting it into small pieces, and putting it into cask through the bung-holes. In the first instance, the ship must be moored to a convenient piece of ice, or placed in an open situation, and the sails so reduced as to require no further attention in the event of bad weather occurring. The hold of the ship must be cleared of its superstructure of casks, until the "ground tier," or lowest stratum of casks is exposed, and the ballast-water must be "started," or pumped out of all the casks that are removed upon deck, as well as out of those on the ground tier, which are first prepared for the reception of the blubber. In "breaking out the hold," it is not necessary to lay open more of the ground tier at a time than three or four casks extend in length.

While the line-managers, together with the "skee-man," (the officer who has the direction of operations in the hold,) the cooper, and perhaps a few others, are employed in breaking out the hold, the rest of the crew on the deck arrange all the variety of apparatus used for the preparation of the blubber before it is put into the casks. Of this apparatus, the most considerable part is the "speck-trough," with its appendages. It consists of a kind of oblong box or chest, about twelve feet in length, one and three quarters feet in breadth, and one and a half feet in depth. The speck-trough is fixed upon the deck, as nearly as possible over the place where the casks are to be filled in the hold. A square hole made in its bottom is placed either over the nearest hatchway to the scene of operations, or upon a corresponding hole cut in the deck. The speck-trough is then secured, and its lid turned backwards into an horizontal position. The surface of the lid, forming a level table, is then covered with blocks of whale's-tail from end to end. This substance makes an excellent chopping-block, and preserves the chopping-knives from injury when used for dividing the blubber upon it. Into the square hole in the bottom of the speck-trough is fitted an iron frame, to which is suspended a canvas tube, or "hose," denominated a "lull." The lull is open at both ends. Its diameter is about a foot, and its length sufficient to reach from the deck to the bottom of the hold. To the middle, or towards the upper part of the lull, is attached a "pair of nippers," consisting of two sticks fastened together by a kind of hinge at one end, and capable of being pressed together at the other. The nippers being passed across the body of the lull, and their detached extremities brought together, they embrace it so closely that nothing can pass downward while they remain in this position; but when, on the other hand, the nippers are extended, the lull forms a free channel of communication between the speck-trough and the hold.

Everything being in readiness, the blubber, as it is now thrown out of the flens-gut by the kings, undergoes the following several operations. It is received upon deck by the "krengers," whose office is to remove all the muscular parts, together with such spongy or fibrous fat as is known by experience to produce very little oil. When these substances, which go under the general denomination of kreng, are included among the blubber in the casks, they pass through a kind of fermentation, and generate such a quantity of gas as sometimes to burst the containing vessels, and occasion the loss of their contents. From the krengers the blubber passes to the harpooners. Each of these officers, provided with a blubber-knife, or a strand-knife, places himself by the side of the "closh," fixed in the deck. An attendant, by means of a pair of "hand-hooks," or a "pick-haak," then mounts a piece of blubber upon the spikes of the closh, and the harpooner slices off the skin.

From the skinners, the blubber passes into an open space, called the bank, prepared as a depository in front of the speck-trough, and it is then laid upon the chopping-blocks as wanted. It now falls under the hands of the boat-steerers, who, armed with chopping-knives, are arranged in a line by the side of the chopping-blocks with the speck-trough before them. Thus prepared, they divide the blubber, as it is placed on their blocks, into oblong pieces, not exceeding four inches in diameter, and push it into the speck-trough intended for its reception. And finally, the blubber falls under the direction of the line-managers, stationed in the hold, who receive it into tubs through the lull, and pass it with their hands into the casks, through their bung-holes. When a cask is nearly filled, the packing is completed by the use of a "pricker," one piece after another being thrust in by this instrument until it can contain no more. It is then securely bunged up.

When the ground-tier casks, as far as they have been exposed are filled, the second-tier of casks is stowed upon it, and likewise filled with blubber, together with the third-tier casks when necessary. When fish can be had in sufficiency, the hold is filled and likewise the space between decks. When a ship is deficient in casks, vacancies adapted for the reception of the cargo are filled with blubber in bulk. The operation of making off was in the early ages of the fishery performed on shore, and even so late as the middle of the last century, it was customary for ships to proceed into a harbour, and remain while this process was going on.

In the Greenland whale-fishery, the importance of a code of laws was at a very early period apparent. A fish struck by the people of two different ships became an object of dispute, the first striker claiming the whole, and the second demanding a share for his assistance. Stores saved from wrecked vessels, and especially the cargoes of wrecks, being objects of much moment, were also liable to occasion disputes in a still higher degree. Hence, about the year 1677, the Dutch issued a code of regulations, founded on equitable principles, for the prevention of quarrels and litigation among the fishers. As these were found to be insufficient, the States-General of Holland and West Friesland, in the year 1696, approved and confirmed the general regulations with respect to the saving of the crews and stores of vessels wrecked in the ice, the right to whales under peculiar circumstances, and other matters connected with the fishery. They consisted of twelve articles, and every captain, specksioneer, and officer concerned in the fishery, was obliged to subscribe them. After being duly announced, these articles were enforced by commissioners, chosen from among the principal Greenland owners of Holland, for conducting and carrying into effect this and other matters connected with the prosperity and regulation of the fishery.

Among the British whale-fishers, it does not appear that any particular laws were ever expressly laid down for the adjusting of differences; yet custom has established certain principles as constituting the rule of right, the legality of which is sufficiently acknowledged by their being universally respected. The fundamental articles are two. First, that a fast fish, or a fish in any way in possession, whether alive or dead, is the sole and unquestionable property of the persons so maintaining the connection or possession; and secondly, that a loose fish, alive or dead, is fair game. The first of these regulations can need no modification, but the second can only be recommended for its simplicity and tendency to prevent litigation, since circumstances may, and do, sometimes occur, in which its application is liable to some objection. In this, as in other departments of human conduct, it is impossible by any strict regulations to prevent all kinds of injustice. The highest code of human morals enjoins on men what they shall be, as well as what they shall do, and provides for them the one golden precept, "Whatsoever ye would that men should do to you, do ye even so to them." Conduct, which it is impossible to punish by appeal to any human tribunal, is often most fearfully in violation of this law, and must await the decisions of that day, when God shall try every man's work of what sort it is.

The following circumstance, which occurred a good many years ago, has a tendency to illustrate the existing Greenland laws, and to set them in a prominent light. During a storm of wind and snow, several ships were beating to windward, under easy sail, along the edge of a pack. When the storm abated and the weather cleared, the ships steered towards the ice. Two of the fleet approached it about a mile asunder, abreast of each other, when the crews of each ship accidentally got sight of a dead fish at a little distance, within some loose ice. Each ship now made sail to endeavour to reach the fish before the other, which fish, being loose, would be the prize of the first that should get possession of it. Neither ship could outsail the other, but each continued to press forward toward the prize. The little advantage one of them had in distance, the other compensated with velocity. On each bow of the two ships was stationed a principal officer, armed with a harpoon, in readiness to discharge. But it so happened that the ships came in contact with each other, when within a few yards of the fish, and in consequence of the shock with which their bows met, they rebounded to a considerable distance. The officers at the same moment discharged their harpoons, but all of them fell short of the fish. A hardy fellow, who was second-mate of the leeward ship, immediately leaped overboard, and with great dexterity swam to the whale, seized it by the fin, and proclaimed it his prize. It was, however, so swollen, that he was unable to climb upon it, but was obliged to remain shivering in the water until assistance should be sent. His captain, elated with his good luck, forgot, or at least neglected, his brave second-mate, and before he thought of sending a boat to release him from his disagreeable situation, prepared to moor his ship to an adjoining piece of ice. Meanwhile, the other ship tacked, and the master himself stepped into a boat, pushed off, and rowed deliberately towards the dead fish. Observing the trembling seaman still in the water, holding by the fin, he addressed him with, "Well, my lad, you've got a fine fish here," to which, after a natural reply in the affirmative, he added, "But don't you find it very cold?" "Yes," replied the shivering sailor, "I'm almost starved; I wish you would allow me to come into your boat until ours arrive." This favour needed no second solicitation; the boat approached the man, and he was assisted into it. The fish being again loose and out of possession, the captain instantly struck his harpoon into it, hoisted his flag, and claimed his prize. Mortified and displeased as the other master felt at this trick, for so it certainly was, he had nevertheless no redress, but was obliged to permit the fish to be taken on board of his competitor's ship, and to content himself with abusing the mate for his want of discretion, and with condemning himself for not having more compassion on the poor fellow's feelings, which would have prevented the disagreeable misadventure.

Success in the whale-fishery has been very generally supposed to depend, not upon the exercise of talent and industry on the part of the masters and crews of the fishing-ships, but solely upon the freaks of fortune. That the fishery, however, is altogether a chain of casualties, is as false as it is derogatory to the credit of the persons employed in the enterprise. The most skilful, from adventitious and unavoidable circumstances, may occasionally fail, and the unskilful may be successful; but if we mark the average of a number of years, that is, where the means are equal, a tolerable estimate may be formed of the adventurer's ability, and his fitness for the undertaking in which he is engaged.

The great variety of success, which is observed to result from the exertions of the different Greenland commanders, when the average of several voyages is taken, confirmed the above position, and the circumstance of some masters, in whatever ship they may sail, almost always succeeding, whilst others, however favourably circumstanced, seldom or ever procure a whole cargo, warrants this conclusion, that, most generally, successful fishery depends on the experience, determined perseverance, and personal talent of the master of the vessel, supported by a necessary degree of skill among the people composing his crew. There are occasions, however, especially in those seasons when the Greenland Seas are open, or in some measure free from ice, in which personal talent becomes of comparative little avail. This was strikingly the case in the year 1817, and in some degree in 1818. In the former season, the ice lay at a distance so remote from Spitzbergen, that a space of about two thousand square miles of the surface of the sea, which is usually covered with ice, was wholly void of it. Whatever decisions the judicious fisher was led by experience to form and act upon proved fallacious, and tended only to embarrass him in all his proceedings. The only indication which could be of the least service to the fisher to assist him in the choice of a situation, was the colour of the sea. In places where the water was transparent, and blue, or greenish blue, it was in vain to look for whales, but in a certain stream of cloudy water, of a deep olive-green colour, all the whales which were seen throughout the season, or at least nine-tenths of them, occurred, and the chief part of those which were caught were found in the same stream of water. This kind of sea-water is the favourite resort of whales during the fishing season, evidently because it abounds with various descriptions of *actiniæ*, *sepiæ*, *medusæ*, and *cancri*, which constitute the chief, if not the sole nourishment of the whale.

Success in the fishery is more certain in close than in open seasons, and has some dependence on the suitable equipment of the ships employed in the trade, on a sufficient apparatus, and frequently in no inconsiderable degree on that valuable property of the ship called fast-sailing. When any opening occurs in the ice of a tempting appearance, it frequently happens that a number of ships enter it together. The fastest sailers lead the way, and often procure a whale or two or more before the heavy sailing ships can perform a navigation, and by the time the latter accomplish it, the run of fish is frequently over. Not a little depends in the fishery on the confidence the sailors have in the skill of their captain, and the efficiency of the personal talents and exertions of their officers. If the officers are generally unsuccessful, they are apt to lose confidence in them, and proceed, even when good opportunities occur, without spirit to the attack. The greater their spirits and confidence are, the greater is the probability of their success. Hence, the crew of a ship which has met with success can generally fish better, and more advantageously under the same circumstances, than the people of a clean ship. For the regulation of the ship's movements, for the choice of a situation, for direction in difficulties, for a stimulus when discouraged, for encouragement when weary, and for a variety of other important matters, the master alone must be looked to, on whom, indeed, almost every considerable effort of judgment or forethought devolves.

I now subjoin a few instances of the dangers which accompany the whale-fishery, most of which presented themselves within the sphere of my own observation. Those employed in the occupation of killing whales are, when actually engaged, exposed to danger from three sources, namely, from the ice, from the climate, and from the whales themselves. Of these, the casualties on the ice are the most uncommon, and the least fatal; those from the climate the most fatal, but not the most frequent; and the whale itself is the source of a great proportion of the accidents which occur.

The following instance illustrates the danger from overhanging masses of ice falling on the boats. The crew of one of the Hull whalers, having killed a fish by the side of an iceberg in Davis's Strait, the fins were lashed together, and the tail secured to a boat in the usual way, but by the efforts only of one boat's crew, all the other boats belonging to the same ship being engaged in the capture of two more whales, neither of which were yet subdued. This circumstance occasioned some altercation among the crew of the boat, as to the propriety of their remaining by the dead whale, or of quitting it, and proceeding in an empty boat which was at hand to the assistance of their companions. The latter measure was carried, but as it was deemed expedient that one man should remain in the boat, to which none of them would consent, they were under the necessity of either remaining in idleness by the fish, or leaving the fish and the boat by themselves. But every one being anxious to participate in the more active exercises of the fishery, they at length agreed unanimously to quit the boat connected with the dead fish, and to proceed to the aid of their comrades. The arrangements were just accomplished in time, for they had not rowed many fathoms from the place before a tremendous crash of the berg ensued, an immense mass of ice fell upon the boat they had just quitted, and neither it nor the fish was ever seen afterwards.

Another danger arises from ice when boats are inclosed and beset, and their crews prevented from joining their ships. On June 17th, 1813, several Greenland fishing-ships penetrated the ice into an enticing opening, in which a number of whales were sporting in fancied security. The John, of Greenock,

Neptune, of Aberdeen, Earl Percy, of Kirkcaldy, were immediately, to appearance, successful. The crew of the John in a short time killed several fish; the people of the Neptune killed one, and struck a second; and the crew of the Earl Percy struck one also. Things were in this state when I arrived in the same situation with the Esk. My harpooners, happily as it proved, did not succeed in any measure. The sea was as smooth as the surface of a pond, but the ice I observed was in a strange state of disturbance. Some floes, and some large pieces, moved with a velocity of three to four miles per hour, while other similar masses were at rest. The John, which, on her first arrival in this situation, had navigated an open lake some leagues in circumference, was in the space of a few hours closely beset. The captain of the Neptune, alarmed by the danger to which his men and boats were exposed, left his ship to the care of his second-mate, with eleven or twelve men, and proceeded himself in a boat, making the fifth, to their assistance. In a few minutes, these five boats, together with two belonging to the Earl Percy, were closely fixed in the ice. The ships were forced to a distance; the ice in the course of the following morning spread to the width of seven or eight miles, and shortly afterwards the people in the boats and those in the corresponding ships lost sight of each other.

My father, who at this time commanded the John, had anticipated the consequences of the ice closing, and found refuge in a cove in an adjoining field filled with bay-ice, into which he thrust his ship, and obtained shelter for himself and his comrades who were thus beset. After three days, the ice slackened, and the Neptune boats, together with those belonging to the Earl Percy, left the John, although neither the sea nor their ships were visible. In this adventure they proved successful. When they had rowed many hours to the south-eastward, they discovered a ship, on their approach to which they were invited on board, and received some refreshment. After this, having received information of the relative situation of their ships, they put off, and soon after had the happiness of regaining their respective vessels. This circumstance, which was the occasion of so much anxiety, danger, and loss of time to the crews of the Neptune and Earl Percy, proved the contrary to the people of the John, as they added to her cargo seventeen whales, within the space of five days, and on the sixth, the ice having again slackened, they made their escape into a place of safety.

The climate of the Polar regions becomes a source of danger to the whale-fishers when boats are separated from the ship to which they belong, in foggy weather when they are overtaken by a storm and prevented from joining their ship, and when the people in the boats are long exposed to inclement winds.

On the commencement of a heavy gale of wind, May 11th, 1813, fourteen men put off in a boat from the Volunteer, of Whitby, with the view of setting an anchor in a large piece of ice, to which it was their intention to moor the ship. The ship approached; on a signal being made the sails were clewed up, and a rope fixed to the anchor, but the ice shivering with the violence of the strain, when the ship fell astern the anchor flew out, and the ship went adrift. The sails being again set, the ship was reached to the eastward, (wind at north,) the distance of about two miles, but in attempting to wear and return, the ship, instead of performing the evolution, scudded a considerable distance to leeward, and was then reached out to sea, thus leaving fourteen of her crew to a fate most dreadful, the fulfilment of which seemed inevitable. The temperature of the air was 15° or 16° of Fahrenheit, when these poor men were left upon a detached piece of ice, without food, without shelter from the inclement storm, and deprived of every means of refuge, except in a single boat, which, on account of the number of men, and violence of the storm, was incapable of conveying them to their ship. Death stared them in the face whichever way they turned, and a division in opinion ensued.

Some were wishful to remain by the ice, but the ice could afford them no shelter from the piercing wind, and would probably be soon broken to pieces by the increasing swell; others were anxious to attempt to join their ship, while she was yet in sight, but the force of the wind, the violence of the sea, and the smallness of the boat in comparison of the number of men to be conveyed, were objections which would have appeared utterly insurmountable to any persons but men in a state of despair. Judging that by remaining on the ice death was but retarded for a few hours, as the extreme cold must eventually benumb their faculties, and invite a sleep which would overcome the remains of animation, they determined on making the attempt to row to their ship. Poor creatures! what must have been their sensations at this moment, when the spark of hope yet remaining was so feeble that a premature death even to themselves seemed inevitable. They made the daring experiment, when a few minutes' trial convinced them that the attempt was utterly impracticable. They then, with longing eyes, turned their efforts towards recovering the ice they had left, but their utmost exertions were unavailing. Every one now viewed his situation as desperate, and anticipated as certain the fatal event that was to put a period to his life. How great must have been their delight, and how overpowering their sensations, when, at this most critical juncture, a ship appeared in sight! She was advancing directly towards them; their voices were extended, and their flag displayed. But although it was impossible they should be heard, it was not impossible they should be seen. Their flag was descried by the people on board the ship, their courses were so directed as to form the speediest union, and in a few minutes they found themselves on the deck of the Lively, of Whitby, under circumstances of safety. They received from their townsmen the warmest congratulations, and while each individual was forward in contributing his assistance towards the restoration of their benumbed bodies, each of the rescued appeared sensible that their narrow escape from death was highly providential.

The forbearance of God is wonderful. Perhaps these very men a few hours before were impiously invoking their own destruction, or venting imprecations upon their fellow-beings. True it is, the goodness of the Almighty extendeth over all his works, and that while "he delighteth in mercy" he is "slow to anger." It is no exaggeration to affirm, that every guilty soul of man unpardoned and uncleansed through the blood of the Mediator, is exposed to a peril equally portentous with that which threatened these fishermen. God has, however, provided an ark of mercy, floating on the billows of life's tempestuous, dangerous ocean, within which every soul may find perfect and permanent peace. That ark is even now present, and entrance to it may be instantly secured. To delay is to increase the peril, perhaps beyond the possibility of future relief. "Behold, now is the accepted time; behold, now is the day of salvation." Reader, enter into this ark of mercy by faith in the Lord Jesus!

One of the most calamitous events which in modern times has occurred in the fishery, was that which happened to the crew of the Ipswich, captain Gordon, about fifteen years ago. A whale was struck and killed by the Ipswich's people early in the spring of the year, a season in which the weather is most uncertain. A storm commenced, accompanied with snow, before the capture was completed, but nevertheless the fish was taken to the ship, and having shelter from the ice it was flensed. Meanwhile, four boats' crews were employed on a piece of ice, in hauling in the lines of the fast-boats, etc., during the performance of which duties the ship drifted out of sight of them. Every effort was then made by the captain for discovering these unhappy men, who, being above twenty in number, constituted nearly half of his crew. But the weather continuing thick and stormy, and the frost most intense, it is probable that they all perished before the conclusion of the gale; at least none of them were saved, nor can I learn that any of their bodies were ever found.

The remarkable property of oil in smoothing the surface of the sea when considerably agitated, and of preventing breakers in the main ocean, was sometimes resorted to by the ancient whale-fishers for their preservation, when overtaken by storms at sea. It was not unusual, I believe, a century ago, for every whale-boat to carry along with it a keg of oil for this very purpose; which oil, being slowly poured overboard in a storm, afforded a sort of defence to the boat as it drifted to leeward. The height of the waves, it is true, is not affected by the action of the oil, but as it intercepts the attraction which dry air possesses for water, it prevents the immediate action of the wind, quells the ruffled surface of the waves, and in a great degree prevents the tendency to breakers, which constitutes the principal danger in a storm.

The most extensive source of danger to the whale-fisher, when actively engaged in his occupation, arises from the object of his pursuit. The fisher is liable to receive contusions from oars forcibly struck by the fish, or from direct blows from its fins or tail; he is liable to accidents from getting entangled by the lines, or from the boat being drawn under water by the fish through the medium of the lines; and he is in danger of being thrown overboard by the heeling or jerking of the boat, or more particularly from the boat being stove, upset, sunk, or projected into the air, by the force of a blow from the whale.

One of the crew of the John, of Greenock, who was in a fast-boat in the fishery of 1818, unfortunately slipped his foot through a coil of line in the act of running out, which drew him forward to the boat's stern, and separated his foot by the ancle. He was conveyed by the first boat to the ship, where the assistance of several surgeons being procured, the lower part of the leg was cut off. After this, the poor fellow, having received the most unremitting attention from captain Jackson, with the best sustenance and accommodation the ship could afford, was restored to health, and his wound nearly healed before the conclusion of the voyage. It is worthy of being remarked, that the captain and crew of the John subscribed upwards of £24 for his relief, which was increased by the owners of the ship and others, on arrival, to about £37. This sum was placed in the "Provident Bank," at Greenock, from whence he was permitted to draw it, after the rate of 7s. per week.

A harpooner, belonging to the Henrietta, of Whitby, when engaged in lancing a whale, into which he had previously struck a harpoon, incautiously cast a little line under his feet that he had just hauled into the boat, after it had been drawn out by the fish. A painful stroke of his lance induced the whale to dart suddenly downward, his line began to run out from beneath his feet, and in an instant caught him by a turn round his body. He had but just time to call out, "Clear away the line!" — "Oh dear!" when he was almost cut asunder, dragged overboard, and drowned. The line was cut at the moment, but without avail. The fish descended a considerable depth and died, from whence it was drawn to the surface by the lines connected with it, and secured.

On the 3rd of June, 1811, a boat from the ship Resolution, commanded at the time by myself, put off in pursuit of a whale, and was rowed upon its back. At the moment that it was harpooned, it struck the side of the boat a violent blow with its tail, the shock of which threw the boat-steerer to some distance into the water. A repetition of the blow projected the harpooner and line-manager in a similar way, and completely drenched the part of the crew remaining in the boat with the sprays. One of the men regained the boat, but, as the fish immediately sank and drew the boat away from the place, his two companions in misfortune were soon left far beyond the reach of assistance. The harpooner, though a practised swimmer, felt himself so bruised and enervated by a blow he had received on the chest, that he was totally incapacitated from giving the least support to his fellow-sufferer. The ship being happily near, a boat, which had been lowered on the first alarm, arrived to their succour at the moment when the line-manager, who was unacquainted with the art of swimming, was on the point of sinking to rise no more. Both the line-manager and harpooner were preserved; and the fish, after a few hours' close pursuit, was subdued.

While the same ship navigated an open lake of water in the 81° north lat., during a keen frost and strong north wind, on the 2nd of June, 1806, a whale appeared, and a boat put off in pursuit. On its second visit to the surface of the sea it was harpooned. A convulsive heave of the tail which succeeded the wound struck the boat at the stern, and, by its reaction, projected the boat-steerer overboard. As the line in a moment dragged the boat beyond his reach, the crew threw some of their oars towards him for his support, one of which he happily seized. The ships and boats being at a considerable distance, and the fast-boat being rapidly drawn away from him, the harpooner cut the line, with the view of rescuing him from his dangerous situation. But no sooner was this act performed than, to their extreme mortification, they discovered, in consequence of some oars being thrown towards their floating comrades, and others being broken or unshipped by the blow from the fish, one oar only remained, with which, owing to the force of the wind, they tried in vain to approach him. A considerable period elapsed before any boat from the ship could afford him assistance, though the men strained every nerve for the purpose. At length, when they reached him, he was found with his arms stretched over an oar, almost deprived of sensation. On his arrival at the ship he was in a deplorable condition. His clothes were frozen like mail, and his hair constituted a helmet of ice. He was immediately conveyed into the cabin, his clothes taken off, his limbs and body dried and well rubbed, and a cordial administered to him. A dry shirt and stockings were then put upon him, and he was laid in the captain's bed. After a few hours' sleep, he awoke, and appeared considerably relieved. He complained of a painful sensation of cold. He was therefore removed to his own berth, and one of his messmates ordered to lie on each side of him, whereby the diminished circulation of the blood was accelerated, and the animal heat restored. The shock on his constitution, however, was greater than was anticipated. He recovered in the course of a few days so as to be able to engage in his ordinary pursuits, but many months elapsed before his countenance exhibited its wonted appearance of health.

A remarkable instance of the power which the whale possesses in its tail was exhibited within my own observation, in the year 1807. On the 29th of May, a whale was harpooned by an officer belonging to the Resolution. It descended a considerable depth, and on its reappearance evidenced an uncommon degree of irritation. It made such a display of its fins and tail, that few of the crew were hardy enough to approach it. The captain, (my father,) observing their timidity, called a boat, and himself struck the second harpoon. Another boat immediately followed, and, unhappily, advanced too far. The tail was again reared into the air in a terrific attitude. The impending blow was evident. The harpooner, who was directly underneath, leaped overboard. At the next moment, the threatened stroke was impressed on the centre of the boat, which buried it in the water. Happily no one was injured. The harpooner, who leaped overboard, escaped certain death by the act, the tail having struck the very spot on which he stood. The effects of the blow were astonishing. The keel was broken, the gunwales and every plank, excepting two, were cut through, and it was evident the boat would have been completely divided had not the tail struck directly upon a coil of lines. The boat was rendered useless.

The Dutch ship, Gort-Moolen, commanded by Cornelius Gerard Ouwekaas, with a cargo of seven fish, was anchored in Greenland, in the year 1660. The captain, perceiving a whale ahead of his ship, beckoned his attendants, and threw himself into a boat. He was the first to approach the whale, and succeeded in harpooning it before the arrival of the second boat, which was on the advance. Jacques Vienkes, who had the direction of it, joined his captain immediately afterwards, and prepared to make a second attack on the fish when it should remount to the surface. At the moment of its ascension, the boat of Vienkes happening unhappily to be perpendicularly above it, was so suddenly and forcibly lifted up by a stroke of the head of the whale, that it was dashed to pieces before the harpooner could discharge his weapon. Vienkes flew along with the pieces of the boat, and fell upon the back of the animal. This intrepid seaman, who still retained his weapon in his grasp, harpooned the whale on which he stood, and by means of the harpoon and the line, which he never abandoned, he steadied himself firmly upon the fish, notwithstanding his hazardous situation, and regardless of a considerable wound that he received in his leg, in his fall along with the fragments of the boat. All the efforts of the other boats to approach the whale and deliver the harpooner were futile. The captain, not seeing any other method of saving his companion, who was in some way entangled with the line, called to him to cut it with his knife, and betake himself to swimming. Vienkes, embarrassed and disconcerted as he was, tried in vain to follow this counsel. His knife was in the pocket of his drawers, and, being unable to support himself with one hand, he could not get it out. The whale meanwhile continued advancing along the surface of the water with great rapidity, but happily never attempted to dive. While his comrades despaired of his life, the harpoon by which he held at length disengaged itself from the body of the whale. Vienkes, being then liberated, did not fail to take advantage of this circumstance. He cast himself into the sea, and, by swimming, endeavoured to regain the boats which continued the pursuit of the whale. When his shipmates perceived him struggling with the waves, they redoubled their exertions. They reached him just as his strength was exhausted, and had the happiness of rescuing this adventurous harpooner from his perilous situation.

In one of my earliest voyages to the whale-fishery, I observed a circumstance which excited my highest astonishment. One of our harpooners had struck a whale; it dived, and all the assisting boats had collected round the fast-boat before it rose to the surface. The first boat which approached it advanced incautiously upon it. It rose with unexpected violence beneath the boat, and projected it and all its crew to the height of some yards in the air. It fell on its side, upset, and cast all the men into the water. One man received a severe blow in his fall, and appeared to be dangerously injured; but, soon after his arrival on board of the ship, he recovered from the effects of the accident. The rest of the boat's crew escaped without any hurt.

Captain Lyons, of the Raith, of Leith, while prosecuting the whale-fishery on the Labrador coast, in the season of 1802, discovered a large whale at a short distance from the ship. Four boats were dispatched in pursuit, and two of them succeeded in approaching it so closely together, that two harpoons were struck at the same moment. The fish descended a few fathoms in the direction of another of the boats, which was on the advance, rose accidentally beneath it, struck it with its head, and threw the boat, men, and apparatus, about fifteen feet into the air. It was inverted by the stroke, and fell into the water with its keel upwards. All the people were picked up alive by the fourth boat, which was just at hand, excepting one man, who, having got entangled in the boat, fell beneath it, and was drowned. The fish was soon afterwards killed.

When a ship has on board an ample cargo, or when the fogs set in, and the whales totally disappear, so as to put a period to the fishery for that season, there remains no sufficient motive to induce further stay in the country; the course of each ship is therefore directed immediately homeward. On the arrival of a fishing-ship at the port from whence she sailed, the mustering-officer of the customs repairs on board, receives the manifest of the cargo, (which is a kind of schedule in writing, containing all particulars respecting it,) with a true copy thereof, examines into the identity and number of the crew, by the usual form of mustering, and places an officer or two on board, to take charge of the cargo on the part of the revenue. The duty of these officers is to take account of every cask or other article of which the cargo consists, as it is discharged from the ship, and one of them accompanies the same to its destination, carrying an account thereof in writing, and not quitting the lighter, wherein it is contained, until he is relieved by another officer, who is placed in the capacity of landing-waiter on the premises where the blubber is warehoused or boiled.

Within twenty-four hours after the ship arrives in port, the master is required, under the penalty of one hundred pounds, to attend at the custom-house to make his report; that is, to make affidavit of the built, burden, and cargo of the ship he commands; on which occasion he must deliver his manifest to the collector or other chief officer, (if it has not before been demanded of him,) under the penalty of two hundred pounds. At the same time, the log-book must be produced, and its contents, as required by law, verified on the oath of the master and mate, and affidavit also made by the same persons of their faithful dealings according to the requirements of the law during the voyage. After these things are accomplished, the mustering-officer's certificate and schedule of the crew, the commissioners' license, and the affidavits of master and mate are transmitted to the commissioners, who, being satisfied of the faithfulness of all the proceedings, are required to order payment of the bounty on demand.

Previous to the cargo being admitted to entry, free from the duties imposed on the produce of foreign fishery, the owner, importer, or consignee of the cargo, together with the master or commander of the vessel, must severally make oath, each to the best of his knowledge and belief, that the said cargo was the produce of fish, etc., actually caught by the crew of a British-built vessel, wholly owned by her Majesty's subjects, usually residing in Great Britain, etc., registered and navigated according to law. The importer or consignee of any goods imported into Britain is required, within twenty days after the master should have made his report, under certain penalties, to make a due entry with the collector or other chief officer of the customs, at the port where the ship shall arrive, of all the goods by him imported therein, and pay the full duties thereon.

CHAPTER IV
ACCOUNT OF THE DAVIS'S STRAIT WHALE-FISHERY, WITH STATEMENTS OF EXPENSES AND PROFITS OF A FISHING-SHIP

Ships intended for Davis's Strait commonly put to sea a little earlier than the Greenland ships. Some years ago, they were in the habit of sailing in the latter part of February, but at present they seldom leave their ports before the beginning or middle of March. On their passage outward, the Davis's Strait fishers usually touch at Orkney or Shetland, for the purpose of procuring men, and such trifling stores as are furnished at a cheap rate in these islands, together with a view of trimming and preparing their vessels for accomplishing the passage across the Atlantic. In consequence of the frequent storms and high seas which prevail in the spring of the year, the passage across the Atlantic is often attended with difficulty. The whalers are constantly liable to meet with icebergs, after passing the meridian of Cape Farewell, up to their arrival at the face of the ice connected with the shore of Labrador. In the night, or in thick weather, they are particularly hazardous, and especially in storms. In moderate winds, indeed, such an intimation of their proximity is to be obtained, either from their natural effulgence in some states of the atmosphere, or from their intense blackness in others, that they can be generally avoided. But in storms, when the ship ceases to be under command, they become one of the most appalling dangers which can be presented to the navigator.

Two most fatal shipwrecks occurred in the Davis's Strait fleets; the Royalist, captain Edmonds, and the London, captain Matthews, were lost, with all hands; the former among icebergs, in 1814, and the latter, as it is supposed, in a similar way, in 1817. Captain Bennet, of the Venerable, was in company with the Royalist immediately before she was wrecked. They fell in with drift-ice at eight a.m., April the 14th, when a heavy gale of wind commenced, and continued twelve hours, after which the wind abated, but suddenly veering to the north-west, a tremendous storm arose, which, accompanied with sleet and snow, continued without intermission during twenty hours. Before dark of the 15th, (nautical day,) captain Bennet saw several icebergs, at which time he believed the Royalist was lying to windward of an extensive chain of these islands of ice, among which she was wrecked in the course of the same night. The crew probably perished immediately, as the sea was uncommonly high. In the case both of the Royalist and the London subscriptions were generously opened at Hull, by the owners of the whalers, for the relief of the bereaved relatives of the crew.

The fishery on the coast of Labrador commences occasionally in the month of March. On this station, which is inhabited by a large description of whales, some fishers have persevered altogether, and have sometimes procured great cargoes. It is, however, a dangerous fishery. The nights being long and dark on their first arrival, they are obliged to use lanterns in their boats, when fish happen to be struck, or to remain unsubdued at close of day, for the purpose of keeping the ships and boats together; on which occasions the stormy weather that frequently occurs at this season exposes them to continued danger. Those who prosecute the northern fishery, after making the ice at the "south-west," as the neighbourhood of the Labrador coast is usually denominated, proceed almost immediately up Davis's Strait towards Baffin's Bay. If in the month of April or beginning of May they commence this navigation, and sail along the edge of the western ice to the northward, they often find it joining the ice connected with the west coast of Greenland, in the latitude 66½° or 67°, and meet with a considerable barrier of it in 68°, immediately beyond which, a few leagues from land, is a good fishing-station. As the ice opens to the northward, the whales retreat in that direction, and the fishers follow as promptly as possible. The whalers often reach Disko early in May, but it is generally the latter end of this month, or the beginning of June, before they can pass the second barrier of ice, lying about Hare Island, in the 71st degree of latitude, and enter the northern inlets frequented by the whales. The three inlets called the South-east Bay, Jacob's Bight, and the North-east Bay, were most productive fishing-stations some years ago, but of late they have afforded but few whales. From hence, if no fish are found, the whalers proceed to the western part of the strait, towards Cumberland Island, or persevere along the east side of Davis's Strait towards Baffin's Bay, to the eastern parts of which the fish appear to retreat as the season advances, and as the ice clears away from the northern and eastern shores.

In Baffin's Bay, and in the inlets of West Greenland, the fishery is conducted under the most favourable circumstances. The water being shallow in many situations, the boats require only a small quantity of line, and the weather being warm, the sailors perform their operations, if not with pleasure, at least with comfort to themselves. But at the south-west, each operation of the fishery is performed under rather unpleasant and even dangerous circumstances. Darkness of night, exposure to storms, and frequency of swells, are all unfavourable to the fishers. The flensing of a whale at the south-west is usually more troublesome and more hazardous than elsewhere, owing to the prevalent swell, which rarely altogether subsides.

Davis's Strait fishers, within the present century, after making a successful fishery at a distance from land, have been in the habit of resorting to the bays, there mooring in safety, until the troublesome process of making-off was accomplished. On the passage homewards, the ships usually steer down the middle of the strait, and proceed sufficiently far south for avoiding the "Cape-ice," before they haul up to the eastward. From thence, the prevalence of westerly winds in the summer season generally affords them an easy passage across the Atlantic. The legislative regulations on the importation of Davis's Strait produce are the same as on cargoes obtained in the Greenland fishery.

Among the Dutch fishers, we find that, during a period of a hundred and seven years, included between 1669 and 1778, each ship in a fleet of a hundred and thirty-two sail, which proceeded annually to Greenland, afforded to the owners, on an average, a profit of 3,126 florins; and that, in a period of sixty years, ending with 1778, a fleet of fifty-three ships, which sailed annually to Davis's Strait, realized to the owners a profit of 3,469 florins per voyage; thus exceeding the produce of the Greenland fishery by 343 florins on each ship, per voyage, after ample allowance is made for the greater length of the voyage to Davis's Strait, together with the additional wear and tear. Among the British fishers, the advantage seems also to have been on the side of Davis's Strait, particularly of late years. But if we deduct the value of skins taken by the Greenland fishers, but not estimated in their cargoes, say £20 to £30 per ship, and the additional expenses of a Davis's Strait voyage, occasioned by the greater wear and tear, and the provisions and wages for a voyage, longer by one or two months than that to Greenland, we shall reduce the balance in favour of the Davis's Strait fishers to a very small sum.

During the four years, ending with 1817, the amount of the cargoes of the British Greenland whale-fishing ships, (consisting of three hundred and seventy-six sail, repeated voyages included,) was 3,508 whales, which produced 33,070 tuns of oil, and 1,682 tons of whalebone. At the same time, 210 ships employed in the Davis's Strait fishery procured 1,522 whales, yielding 21,438 tuns of oil, and 1,015 tons of whale-fins. It seems worthy of remark, that the whales caught near Spitzbergen afforded a larger proportion of whalebone, compared with the quantity of oil, than the fish of Davis's Strait; the Greenland fish yielding a ton of fins for every 19½ tuns of oil, and the Davis's Strait fish a ton of fins for every 21 tuns of oil. It is remarkable that this should have been the case, when we consider that small fish afford less whalebone than large fish in proportion to their produce in oil, and yet the Greenland fish, which, on the average of four years, were much smaller than those caught in Davis's Strait, have produced the largest proportion of whalebone. The whales taken at the Greenland fishery in four years only average 9½ tuns of oil each, but those caught at Davis's Strait average 14 tuns. It would, therefore, appear that the large whales caught near Spitzbergen are much stouter than those taken in Davis's Strait, and afford such a large proportion of fins as more than compensates for the deficiency in the small whales.

The fluctuating value of shipping renders it difficult to give a fair estimate of the expenses of a whale-ship. The Resolution, of Whitby, burden 219 tons, when new, in the year 1803, cost but £7,791, including all expenses of stores and outfit, premiums of insurance, and advanced money of seamen; while the Esk, of 354 tons of measurement, launched and fitted out at the same port in 1813, cost about £14,000. The ship Resolution was sold in eight shares, and the sums subscribed by the owners and deposited in the hands of the managing owners was £8,000. The balance in favour of the owners of the Resolution for fifteen voyages appeared to be £19,473. 10s. 2d., besides the value of the ship, and the value of the outfit for the sixteenth voyage. If we reckon these at £6,520, the profit derived from £8,000, originally advanced, in addition to the interest of the capital embarked, will amount to £26,000, notwithstanding the last three voyages were but indifferent, of which sum £25,200 has actually been divided. It is, however, necessary to mention, that the Resolution, in her first ten voyages, procured six hundred or seven hundred tuns of oil above the average of the fishery during that period, if not more.

The usual expenses of a Greenland voyage, including outfit, when no cargo is obtained, may be stated at £2,200, exclusive of interest of capital and wear and tear. For every ten tuns of oil procured, there will be an additional expense of £80 or £90 for discharging and boiling the cargo, for oil money and fish money, and for other extraordinaries connected with a successful fishing. Thus the expense of a ship, with a cargo of two hundred tuns of oil, will be at least £4,000.

CHAPTER V
METHOD OF EXTRACTING OIL AND PREPARING WHALE-BONE, WITH A DESCRIPTION OF THESE ARTICLES, AND REMARKS ON THE USES TO WHICH THE SEVERAL PRODUCTS OF THE WHALE-FISHERY ARE APPLIED

On the margin of the river, wet dock, canal, or other sheet of water, communicating with that wherein the whale-fishing ship discharges her cargo, are usually provided the necessary premises for reducing the blubber into oil, consisting commonly of the following articles.

1. A copper vessel or boiler, three to six, or even ten or more tuns' capacity, of a circular form in the horizontal view, and elliptical in the perpendicular section, is fixed at the elevation of six to ten feet above the ground, provided with an appropriate furnace, and covered with a tiled or slated shed.

2. On the same, or on a little lower level than that of the copper, is fixed a square or oblong back or cooler, built of wood generally, capable of containing from ten to twenty tuns of oil, or upwards. Adjoining to this is another back, sometimes a third, and occasionally a fourth or fifth, each placed a little lower than the one preceding it, so that the lowest shall stand with its base about two or three feet above the level of the ground. In some very modern *works*, the coolers are all fixed at the same elevation. Each of the backs is provided with one or more stop-cocks on the most accessible side, for convenience in drawing the oil off into casks.

3. Altogether above the level of the copper, and immediately adjoining it, on the side directed towards the river or canal, an oblong wooden cistern, called the "starting-back," is usually erected, for containing blubber, which ought to be a vessel of equal, or nearly equal, capacity to that of the copper. It is generally provided with a crane, which, with a winch, or other similar

engine attached, is so contrived as to take casks either from the quay, or from a lighter by the side of the quay, and convey them at once to the top of the starting-back. Over this vessel is extended a kind of railing or "gauntree," on which the casks rest without being injured, and are easily movable.

4. The starting-back being elevated two or three yards above the level of the ground, occasionally admits of a "fenk-back," or depository, for the refuse of the blubber, immediately beneath it; which fenk-back is sometimes provided with a *clough* on the side next the water, for "starting" the fenks into a barge or lighter placed below.

5. The premises likewise comprise a *shed* for the cooper, and sometimes a cooper's, or master-boiler's, dwelling-house; the inhabitant of which takes the charge of all the blubber, oil, whalebone, and other articles deposited around him.

6. Warehouses for containing the oil after it is drawn off into casks are also used, not only for preserving it in safe custody, but for defending the casks from the rays of the sun, otherwise they are apt to pine and become leaky, and,

7. Sometimes "steeping-backs" and apparatus for preparing whalebone are comprised within the same inclosure.

The blubber, which was originally in the state of fat, is found, on arrival in a warm climate, to be in a great measure resolved into oil. The casks, containing the blubber, are conveyed, by the mechanical apparatus above mentioned, to the top of the starting-back, into which their contents are emptied or *started* through the bungholes. When the copper is properly cleansed, the contents of the starting-back, on lifting a clough at the extremity, or turning a stop-cock, fall directly into the copper, one edge of which is usually placed beneath. The copper is filled within two or three inches of the top, a little space being requisite to admit of the expansion of the oil when heated; and then a brisk fire is applied to the furnace, and continued until the oil begins to boil. This effect usually takes place in less than two hours. Many of the fritters or fenks float on the surface of the oil before it is heated, but after it is "boiled off," the whole, or nearly so, subside to the bottom. From the time the copper begins to warm until it is boiled off, or ceases to boil, its contents must be incessantly stirred by means of a pole, armed with a kind of broad, blunt chisel, to prevent the fenks from adhering to the bottom or sides of the vessel. When once the contents of the copper boil, the fire in the furnace is immediately reduced, and shortly afterwards altogether withdrawn. Some persons allow the copper to boil an hour, others during two or three hours. The former practice is supposed to produce finer and paler oil, the latter a greater quantity. The same copper is usually boiled twice in every twenty-four hours, Sundays excepted. After the oil has stood to cool and subside, the "bailing" process commences. One of the backs or coolers having been prepared for the reception of the oil, by putting into it a quantity of water, for the double purpose of preventing the heat of the oil from warping or rending the back, and for receiving any impurities which it may happen to hold in suspension, a wooden spout, with a large square box-like head, which head is filled with brushwood or broom, that it may act as a filter, is then placed along from "the copper-head" to the cooler, so as to form a communication between the two. The oil in the copper being now separated from the fenks, water, and other impurities, all of which have subsided to the bottom, is in a great measure run off through the pipe communicating with the cooler, and the remainder is carefully lifted in copper or tin ladles, and poured upon the broom in the spout, from whence it runs into the same cooler, or any other cooler, at the pleasure of the "boilers."

Besides oil and fenks, the blubber of the whale likewise affords a considerable quantity of watery liquor, produced probably from the putrescence of the blood, on the surface of which some of the fenks, and all the greasy animal matter, called foot-je, or footing, float, and upon the top of these the oil. Great care therefore is requisite, on approaching these impure substances, to take the oil off by means of shallow tinned iron or copper ladles, called "skimmers," without disturbing the refuse and mixing it with the oil. There must always, however, be a small quantity towards the conclusion, which is a mixture of oil and footing; such is put into a cask or other suitable vessel by itself, and when the greasy part has thoroughly subsided, the most pure part is skimmed off and becomes fine oil, and the impure is allowed to accumulate by itself, in another vessel, where in the end it affords "brown-oil." From a ton, or 252 gallons by measure of blubber, there generally arises from fifty to sixty gallons of refuse, whereof the greater part is a watery fluid. The constant presence of this fluid, which boils at a much lower temperature than the oil, prevents the oil itself from boiling, which is probably an advantage, since, in the event of the oil being boiled, some of the finest and most inflammable parts would fly off in the form of vapour, whereas the principal part of the steam, which now escapes, is produced from the water. Some persons make a practice of adding a quantity of water, amounting perhaps to half a tun, to the contents of each copper, with the view of weakening or attenuating the viscid impurities contained in the blubber, and thus obtaining a finer oil; others consider the quantity of watery fluid already in the blubber, as sufficient for producing every needful effect.

Each day, immediately after the copper is emptied, and while it is yet hot, the men employed in the manufacture of the oil, having their feet defended by strong leathern or wooden shoes, descend into it, and scour it out with sand and water, until they restore the natural surface of the copper wherever it is discoloured. This serves to preserve the oil from becoming high-coloured, which will always be the case when proper cleanliness is not observed.

When prepared and cooled, the oil is in a marketable state, and requires only to be transferred from the coolers into casks, for the convenience of conveyance to any part of the country. Each of the coolers, it has been observed, is furnished with a stop-cock, beneath which there is a platform adapted for receiving the casks. At the conclusion of the process of boiling each vessel's cargo manufactured on the premises, the backs are completely emptied of their contents. To effect this water is poured in, until the lower part of the stratum of oil rises within a few lines of the level of the stop-cock, and permits the greatest part of the oil to escape. The quantity left amounts, perhaps, to half an inch or an inch in depth; to recover this oil without water requires a little address. A deal board, in length a little exceeding the breadth of the cooler, is introduced at one end, diagonally, and placed, edge-ways, in its contents. The ends of the board being covered with flannel, when pressed forcibly against the two opposite sides of the cooler, prevent the oil from circulating past. The board is then advanced slowly forward towards the part of the back where the stop-cock is placed, and, in its progress, all the oil is collected by the board, while the water has a free circulation beneath it. When the oil accumulates to the depth of the board, its further motion is suspended until the oil thus collected is drawn off. Another similar board is afterwards introduced, at the furthest extremity of the cooler, and passed forward in the same manner, whereby the little oil which escapes the first is collected. The remnant is taken up by skimmers. The smell of oil during its extraction is undoubtedly disagreeable; but, perhaps, not more so than the vapour arising from any other animal substance, submitted to the action of heat when in a putrid state. It is an erroneous opinion that a whale-ship must always give out the same unpleasant smell. The fact is, that the fat of the whale, in its fresh state, has no offensive flavour whatever, and never becomes disagreeable until it is brought into a warm climate, and becomes putrid.

Whale-oil, prepared by the method just described, is of a pale honey-yellow colour; but sometimes, when the blubber from which it is procured happens to be of the red kind, the oil appears of a reddish-brown colour. When first extracted, it is commonly thick, but after standing some time a mucilaginous substance subsides, and it becomes tolerably limpid and transparent. Its smell is somewhat offensive, especially when it is long kept. It consists of oil, properly so called, a small portion of spermaceti, and a little gelatine. At the temperature of 40° the latter substances become partially concrete, and make the oil obscure; and at the temperature of 32° render it thick with flaky crystals. It is sold by the tun, of 252 gallons, wine measure. Its specific gravity is 0·9214. The tun weighs 17 cwt. 1 qr. 1 lb. 12 oz. 14 dr. The value of whale-oil, like that of every other similar article, is subject to continual variations. In the year 1744, oil sold in England for £10. 1s. per tun; in 1754, for £29; in 1801, for £50; in 1807, for £21; and in 1813, when the price was the highest ever obtained, for £55 or £60 per tun.

The application of gas, produced by the distillation of coal, for lighting the public streets and buildings, manufactories, shops, etc., which formerly were lighted with oil, it was apprehended would be ruinous to the whale-fishery trade, and certainly had a very threatening appearance; but hitherto, owing to the amount of whale-oil lately imported having been less than the ordinary quantity, this expected effect of the employment of gas-lights has not been felt.

When blubber is boiled in Greenland, the oil produced from it is much brighter, paler, more limpid, and more inflammable than that extracted in Britain. It is also totally free from any unpleasant flavour, and burns without smell. Hence it is evident, that whatever is disagreeable in the effluvia of whale-oil arises from an admixture of putrescent substances. These consist of blood and animal fibre. This latter is the reticulated and cellular fibres of the blubber, wherein the oil is confined, which produces the fenks when boiled. When putrefaction commences, a small portion of the blood contained in the blubber is probably combined with the oil, and the animal fibre, in considerable quantity, is dissolved in it. These substances not only occasion the unpleasant smell common to whale-oil, but, by being deposited on the wick of lamps, in burning, produce upon it a kind of cinder, which, if not occasionally removed, causes a great diminution in the quantity of light. A sample of oil, which I extracted in Greenland, about ten years ago, is still fine, and totally free from rancidity. It has certainly acquired a smell, but is not more unpleasant than that of old Florence oil. Hence, were whale-oil extracted in Greenland before the putrefying process commences, or were any method devised of freeing it from the impurities which combine with it in consequence of this process, it would become not only more valuable for common purposes, but would be applicable to almost every use to which spermaceti oil is adapted. In fact, it would become a similar kind of article.

In performing some experiments on oil in Greenland, during the fishing season of 1818, I adopted a process for refining oil extracted from blubber before the putrefying process commenced, by which I procured a remarkably fine oil. It was nearly colourless, beautifully transparent, and very limpid. This oil retains its transparency, even at a very low temperature. It is more inflammable than spermaceti oil, and so pure, that it will burn longer, without forming a crust on the wick of the lamp, than any other oil with which it has been compared.

Besides the oil produced from blubber by boiling, the whalers distinguish such as oozes from the jawbones of the fish by the name of jawbone oil; and inferior oils, which are discoloured, by the denominations of brown oil and black oil, or bilge oil. Brown oil is produced in the way described in the process of boiling; black or bilge oil is that which leaks out of the casks in the course of the voyage, or runs out of any blubber which may happen to be in bulk, and accumulates in the bottom of the ship. This oil is always very dark coloured, viscous, and possessed of little transparency.

Whalebone, or whalefins, as the substance is sometimes, though incorrectly, named, is found in the mouth of the common Greenland whale, to which it serves as a substitute for teeth. It forms an apparatus most admirably adapted as a filter for separating the minute animals on which the whale feeds from the sea-water in which they exist. The Lawgiver of all the creatures, whether rational or irrational, has fitted them with organization appropriate for the purposes for which they live, and has provided them with all that is needful, according to their rank, for the happiness of their lives. The care which is bestowed upon the animals who do not recognise Him is in unison with that more tender kindness which he has manifested to such as have a mind to meditate on his perfections, and a heart wherewith to love him and adore.

The whalebone is a substance of a horny appearance and consistence, extremely flexible and elastic, generally of a bluish black colour, but not unfrequently striped longitudinally white, and exhibiting a beautiful play of colour on the surface. Internally, it is of a fibrous texture, resembling hair, and the external surface consists of a smooth enamel, capable of receiving a good polish. When taken from the whale, the whalebone consists of laminæ, connected by what is called the gum in a parallel series, and ranged along each side of the mouth of the animal. The laminæ are about three hundred in number, in each side of the head. The length of the longest blade, which occurs near the middle of the series, is the criterion fixed on by the fishers for designating the size of the fish. Its greatest length is about fifteen feet. The two sides or series of the whalebone are connected at the upper part of the head or crown-bone of the fish, within a few inches of each other, from whence they hang downwards, diverging so far as to inclose the tongue between their extremities; the position of the blades with regard to each other resembles a frame of saws in a saw-mill; and, taken altogether, they exhibit in some measure the form and position of the roof of a house. The smaller extremity and interior edge of each blade of whalebone, or the edge annexed to the tongue, are covered with a long fringe of hair, consisting of a similar kind of substance to that which constitutes the interior of the bone. Whale-bone is generally brought from Greenland in the same state as when taken from the fish, after being divided into pieces, comprising ten or twelve laminæ in each. Of late years, the price has usually been fluctuating between £50 and £150 per ton. It becomes more valuable as it increases in length and thickness.

In cleansing and preparing the whalebone, the first operation, if not already done, consists of depriving it of the gum. It is then put into a cistern containing water, till the dirt upon its surface becomes soft. When this effect is sufficiently produced, it is taken out piece by piece, laid on a plank placed on the ground, where the operator stands, and scrubbed or scoured with sand and water, by means of a broom or piece of cloth. It is then passed to another person, who, on a plank or bench, elevated to a convenient height, scrapes the root-end, where the gum was attached, until he produces a smooth surface; he, or another workman, then applies a knife or a pair of shears to the edge, and completely detaches all the fringe of hair connected with it. Another person, who is generally the superintendent of the concern, afterwards receives it, washes it in a vessel of clean water, and removes with a bit of wood the impurities out of the cavity of the root. Thus cleansed, it is exposed to the air and sun, until thoroughly dry, when it is removed into a warehouse or other place of safety and shelter.

Before it is offered for sale, it is usually scrubbed with brushes and hair-cloth, by which the surface receives a polish, and all dirt or dust adhering to it removed; and, finally, it is packed in portable bundles, consisting of about one hundred weight each. The size-bone, or such pieces as measure six feet or upwards in length, are kept separate from the under size, the latter being usually sold at half the price of the former. Each blade being terminated with a quantity of hair, there is sometimes a difficulty in deciding whether some blades of whalebone are size or not. Owing to the diminished value of under-sized bones, and more particularly in consequence of the captain and some of the officers engaged in a fishing-ship having a premium on every size fish, it becomes a matter of some importance in a doubtful case to decide this point. From a decision which, I understand, has been made in a court of law, it is now a generally received rule, that so much of the substance terminating each blade as gives rise to two or more hairs is whalebone; though in fact the hair itself is actually the same substance as that of which the whalebone is composed.

The oil produced from the blubber of the whale, in its most common state of preparation, is used for a variety of purposes. It is used in the lighting of the streets of towns, and the interior of places of worship, houses, shops, manufactories, etc.; it is extensively employed in the manufacture of soft soap, as well as in the preparing of leather and coarse woollen cloths; it is applicable in the manufacture of coarse varnishes and paints, in which, when duly prepared, it affords a strength of body more capable of resisting the weather than paint mixed in the usual way with vegetable oil; it is also extensively used for reducing friction in various kinds of machinery; combined with tar, it is much employed in ship-work, and in the manufacture of cordage, and either simple, or in a state of combination, it is applied to many other useful purposes.

One of the most extensive applications of whale-oil, that for illumination, has suffered a considerable diminution, in consequence of the appropriation of gas from coal to the same purpose. This discovery, brilliant as it is acknowledged to be, which in its first application bore such a threatening aspect against the usual consumption of oil, may be the means of bringing the oil of the whale into more extensive use than it has at any former period been. Whale-oil, in the most inferior qualities, is found to afford a gas which, in point of brilliancy, freeness of smell, and ease of manufacture, is greatly superior to that produced from coal. In places where coal is not very cheap, gas, it seems, can be produced from oil at about the same expense as coal-gas; consequently, the numerous advantages of the former will render it highly preferable. Whale-oil, when free from the incombustible and contaminating animal matters which are usually dissolved in it in consequence of putrefaction, is, then, applicable to a variety of purposes, in which the common oil cannot conveniently be employed. Even in its unrefined state, whale-oil frequently obtains an unmerited bad character for burning, when the fault lies in those who have the charge of the lamps in which it is consumed. Want of proper cleanliness, the use of wicks of too great diameter, and sometimes in a damp state, are common errors inimical to the obtaining of a good light.

The fenks, or ultimate refuse of the blubber of the whale, form an excellent manure, especially in soils deficient in animal matter. Fenks might be used, it is probable, in the manufacture of Prussian blue, and also for the production of ammonia. Footing, which is the finer detached fragments of the fenks, not wholly deprived of oil, may be used as a cheap material in the formation of gas. Whale's tail can be converted into glue, and is extensively used in the manufacture of this article, especially in Holland. It forms, as I have already mentioned, chopping-blocks for the fishers. The jawbones, with the skull or crown-bone of the whale, are the largest found in nature. They are sometimes met with of the length of twenty-five feet. Jawbones are used as the ribs of sheds, and in the construction of arches and posts of gateways.

Whalebone, when softened in hot water, or simply by heating it before a fire, has the property of retaining any shape which may then be given to it, provided it be secured in the required form until it becomes cold. This property, together with its great elasticity and flexibility, renders it capable of being applied to many useful purposes. The first way in which it seems to have been employed was in the stays of ladies. Its application to this purpose was at one period, when the quantity imported was small, so general that it attained, in the wholesale way, the price of £700 per ton. Of late years, however, it has fallen somewhat into disrepute, some ladies preferring to support themselves with plates of steel. There has been for many years an extensive consumption of this article in the manufacture of umbrellas and parasols. The white enamel (found in some specimens of whalebone) has been fabricated into ladies' hats, and a variety of ornamental forms of head-dresses; and the black enamel is employed, in the same way as cane, in the construction of the seats or backs of chairs, gigs, sofas, etc. The hair on the edge of the whalebone answers every purpose of bullock's hair in stuffings for chairs, sofas, settees, carriages, mattresses, cushions, etc. An attempt has been made to build whale-boats of this material, but the great alteration which takes place in its dimensions, in different states of the atmosphere, on account of its ready absorption of moisture, renders it inapplicable. It has been used with a much better effect, in the construction of portmanteaus, travelling-trunks, hygrometers, the ram-rods of fowling-pieces, fishing-rods, the shafts, springs, and wheels of carriages, and various other articles.

CHAPTER VI
NARRATIVE OF PROCEEDINGS ON BOARD THE SHIP ESK, DURING A WHALE-FISHING VOYAGE TO THE COAST OF SPITZBERGEN, IN THE YEAR 1816; PARTICULARLY RELATING TO THE PRESERVATION OF THE SHIP UNDER CIRCUMSTANCES OF PECULIAR DANGER

The ship Esk sailed from Whitby on the 29th of March, 1816. We entered the frigid confines of the Icy Sea, and killed our first whale on the 25th of April. On the 30th of April, we forced into the ice with a favourable wind, and after passing through a large body of it, entered an extensive sea, such as usually lies on the western coast of Spitzbergen at this season of the year, early on the morning of the following day. The wind then blowing hard south south-east, we kept our reach to the eastward until three o'clock in the afternoon, when we unexpectedly met with a quantity of ice, which interrupted our course. We then *wared* by the way of avoiding it, but soon found, though the weather was thick with snow, that we were completely embayed in a situation that was truly terrific.

In the course of fourteen voyages, in which I had before visited this inhospitable country, I passed through many dangers wherein my own life, together with those of my companions, had been threatened; but the present case, where our lives seemed to be at stake for a length of time, exceeding twelve hours, far surpassed in awfulness, as well as actual hazard, anything that I had before witnessed. Dangers which occur unexpectedly and terminate suddenly, though of the most awful description, appear like a dream when they are past; but horrors which have a long continuance, though they in some measure decrease in their effect on the mind by a lengthened contemplation of them, yet they leave an impression on the memory which time itself cannot altogether efface. Such was the effect of the present scene. Whilst the wind howled through the rigging with tempestuous roar, the sea was so mountainous that the mast-heads of some accompanying ships, within the distance of a quarter of a mile, were intercepted and rendered invisible by the swells, and our ship frequently rolled the lee-boats into the water, that were suspended with their keels above the roughtree-rail!

At the same time, we were rapidly approaching a body of ice, the masses of which, as hard as rocks, might be seen at one instant covered with foam, the next concealed from the sight by the waves, and instantly afterwards reared to a prodigious height above the surface of the sea. It is needless to relate the means by which we attempted to keep the ship clear of the threatened danger, because those means were without avail. At eleven P.M. we were close to the ice, when perceiving through the mist an opening a short distance within, we directed the drift of the ship towards it. As we approached the ice, the sails were filled, so that the first blow was received obliquely on the bow, when the velocity of the ship was moderate. In this place the pieces of ice were happily of smaller dimensions; at least, all the larger masses we were able to avoid, so that, after receiving a number of shocks, we escaped without any particular accident into the opening or slack part of the ice above noticed. This opening, as far as we could see, promised a safe and permanent release.

But in this we were grievously disappointed: for, when we attempted to ware the ship, which soon became necessary, she refused to turn round, notwithstanding every effort, in a space which, in ordinary circumstances, would have been far more than sufficient for the evolution. In consequence of this accident, which arose partly from the bad *trim* of the ship, and partly from the great violence of the wind, she fell to leeward into a close body of ice, to which we could see no termination. The Mars, of Whitby, and another vessel, which closely followed us as we penetrated the exterior of the ice, being in better trim than the Esk, performed the evolution with ease, and were in a few minutes out of sight. In this dreadful situation, we lay beating against the opposing ice, with terrible force, daring eight successive hours, all which time I was rocked at the top-gallant mast-head, directing the management of the sails, to avoid the largest masses of ice, any one of which would have perforated the side of the ship. By the blessing of God, we succeeded wonderfully; and at eight a.m., the 2nd of May, gained a small opening, where we contrived to navigate the ship until the wind subsided, and we had the opportunity of forcing into a more commodious place. On examining the ship, we found our only apparent damage to consist in the destruction of most of our rudder works, a few slight bruises on the sides, and a cut on the lower part of the stern of the ship.

From this time, to the 20th of May, the fishery was generally interrupted by the formation of new ice, insomuch that during this interval we killed but one whale, while few of our neighbours succeeded so well. During the succeeding week, we became so fixed that we never moved except occasionally a few yards. The next twelve days were spent in most arduous labour in forcing the ship through the ice. At length, on the 12th of June, we happily escaped, though our companions were, for a short time, all left behind. On the 27th of June, we had secured thirteen fish, and our quantity of oil was about 125 tuns. This was a larger cargo than any ship had procured that we had yet met with, excepting only one. On the 28th, the John, of Greenock, commanded by my brother-in-law, Mr. Jackson, joined us.

After proceeding to the westward, the greater part of the 28th, we arrived at the borders of a compact body of field-ice, consisting of immense sheets of prodigious thickness. As I considered the situation not favourable for fishing, the ship was allowed to drift to the eastward all night. In the morning of the 29th, I found, however, that she was very little removed from the place where she lay when I went to bed. I perceived that the floes, between which there had been extensive spaces, were now in the act of closing; and attempted, by lowering four boats, to tow the ship through an opening at a short distance from us. At the moment when we were about to enter it, it closed. In attempting to get the ship into the safety of an indentation, which appeared calculated to afford a secure retreat, a small piece of ice came athwart her bow, stopped her progress, and she was in a minute afterwards subjected to a considerable squeeze. From none, however, of the pieces of ice around us did we apprehend any danger, particularly as the motion of the ice soon abated. There was a danger, however, on the larboard quarter, of which we were totally unconscious. The piece of ice that touched the ship in that part, though of itself scarcely six yards square, and more than one yard above the water, concealed beneath the surface of the sea, at the depth of ten or twelve feet, a hard pointed projection of ice, which pressed against the keel, lifted the rudder, and caused a damage that had nearly occasioned the loss of the ship. About an hour and a half after the accident, the carpenter, having sounded the pump, discovered to our great concern and amazement a depth of eight and a half feet water in the hold. This was most alarming; with despair pictured in every face, the crew set on the pumps; a signal of distress was at the same time hoisted, and a dozen boats approached us from the surrounding ships. In the space of four hours, the water had lowered to nearly four feet, but one of the pumps becoming useless, and bailing being less effectual than at first, the water once more resumed its superiority and gained upon us.

Something, therefore, was now to be done, to stop, if possible, the influx of the water. As the pumping and bailing could not possibly be continued by our own ship's company, it was necessary to make use of some means to attempt a speedy remedy whilst our assistants were numerous. As there was a probability that a bunch of rope-yarns, straw, or oakum, might enter some of the larger leaks, and retard the influx of water, if applied near the place through the medium of a fothering-sail, (that is, a sail drawn by means of ropes at the four corners, beneath the damaged or leaky part,) we in the meantime prepared a lower studding-sail, by sewing bunches of these materials, which, together with sheets of old thin canvas, whalebone-hair, and a quantity of ashes, fitted it well for the purpose. Thus prepared, it was hauled beneath the damaged place, but not the least effect was yet produced. We set about unrigging the ship, and discharging the cargo and stores, upon a flat place of the floe, against which we had moored, with the intention of turning the ship keel upward. My own sailors were completely worn out, and most of our auxiliaries wearied and discouraged; some of them evinced, by their improper conduct, their wish that the ship should be abandoned. Before putting our plan in execution, we placed twenty empty casks in the hold, to act against a quantity of iron ballast which was in the ship, caulked the dark lights, removed all the dry goods and provisions that would injure with the wet, secured all the hatches, skuttles, companion, etc., then, erecting two tents on the ice, one for sheltering myself, and the other for the crew, we ceased pumping, and permitted the ship to fill. At this crisis, men of whom I had conceived the highest opinion for firmness and bravery greatly disappointed my expectations. Among the whole crew, indeed, scarcely a dozen spirited fellows were to be seen.

As no ship could with propriety venture near us, to assist in turning the Esk over, on account of the hazardous position of the ice around her, we had no other means of attempting this singular evolution than by attaching purchases to the ice from the ship. Everything being prepared, while the water flowed into the ship, I sent our exhausted crew to seek a little rest. For my own part, necessity impelled me to endeavour to obtain some repose. I had already been fifty hours without rest, which unusual exertion, together with the anxiety of mind I endured, caused my legs to swell and become so extremely painful, that I could scarcely walk. Spreading, therefore, a mattress upon a few boards, laid on the snow within one of the tents, notwithstanding the coldness of the situation, and the excessive dampness that prevailed from the constant fog, I enjoyed a comfortable repose of four hours, and arose considerably refreshed.

Immediately afterwards, about three p.m., on the 1st of July, I proceeded with all hands to the ship, which, to our surprise, we found had only sunk a little below the sixteenth mark externally, while the water but barely covered a part of "'tween decks within." Perceiving that it was not likely to sink much further, on account of the buoyancy of the empty casks, and the materials of which the ship was composed, we applied all our purchases, but with the strength of 150 men we could not heel her more than five or six stakes. When thus careened, with the weight of two anchors suspended from the mast, acting with the effect of powerful levers on the ship, I accompanied about 120 men on board. All these being arranged on the high side of the deck, ran suddenly to the lower side, when the ship fell so suddenly on one side that we were apprehensive she was about to upset, but after turning a little way the motion ceased. The tackles on the ice being then hauled tight, the heeling position of the ship was preserved, until we mounted the higher part of the deck, and ran to the lower as before. At length, after a few repetitions of this manœuvre, no impression whatever was produced, and the plan of upsetting the ship appeared quite impracticable.

The situation of the ship being now desperate, there could be no impropriety in attempting to remove the keel and garboard strake, which prevented the application of the fothering, for, whatever might be the result, it could scarcely be for the worse. These incumbrances being removed, the sail for fothering was immediately applied to the place, and a vast quantity of fothering materials thrown into its cavity, when it was fairly underneath. Over this sail we spread a fore-sail, and braced the whole as tight to the ship as the keel-bolts, which yet remained in their horizontal position, would admit. The effect was as happy as we could possibly have anticipated. Some time before all these preparations were completed, our people, assisted by the John's crew, who, after a short rest, had returned to us, put the three pumps and bailing tubs in motion, and applied their energies with such effect that in eleven hours the pumps sucked! In this time, a depth of thirteen feet water was pumped out of the hold, besides the leakage. The John's crew on this occasion exerted themselves with a spirit and zeal which were truly praiseworthy. As the assistance of carpenters was particularly needed, we fired a gun, and repeated our signal of distress, which brought very opportunely two boats, with six men each, from the Prescot, and the same number from our tried friend, Mr. Allen, of the North Britain. As we likewise procured the carpenters of these ships, together with those of the John, they commenced operations by cutting through the ceiling, between two frames of timbers directly across the hold, at the distance of about twenty-six feet from the stern-post; a situation which, we were assured, was on the fore part of the leak, or between the leak and the body of the ship. The timbers in this place were unhappily found so closely connected that we had to cut away part of one of the floors, that we might come at the outside plank, and caulk the crevices between it and the timbers; which operation, on account of the great depth of timber, and the vast flow of water that issued at the ceiling, was extremely difficult, tedious, and disagreeable.

Meanwhile that we had good assistance, I allowed our crew four hours' rest, half of them at a time, for which purpose some of their beds were removed from the ice to the ship. Here, for the first time during four days, they enjoyed their repose; for on account of the cold and damp that prevailed when they rested on the ice, several of them, I believe, never slept. Some of the John's people returning to us, swayed up the top-mast, and rigged most of the yards, while our men were employed stowing the main-hold, which, by the floating of the casks, was thrown into a singular state of disorder. Some of the casks were found without heads, and all the blubber lost, and many were found bilged, or otherwise damaged.

After the carpenters had completely cleared the roomstead—that is, the space between any two ribs or frames of timbers in a ship—they drove oakum into it, along with an improved woollen sheathing substance; and occasionally, where the spaces were very large, pieces of fat pork. The spaces or crevices between the planks of the ceiling and the timber being then filled, all the above substances were firmly driven down by means of pine wedges, and the spaces between each of the wedges caulked. This would have been very complete, had not the increased flow of the water overcome the pumps, and covered the ceiling where the carpenters were at work. They were therefore obliged to wedge up the place with great expedition;

and being at the same time greatly fatigued, the latter part of the operation was accomplished with much less perfection than I could have wished.

Hitherto calm weather, with thick fog, having constantly prevailed, was the occasion of several ships remaining by us and affording assistance, which would otherwise have left us. But the weather having now become clear, and a prospect of prosecuting the fishery being presented, every ship deserted us, except the John, and she was preparing to leave us likewise. In the state of extreme jeopardy in which we were still placed, the love of life, on the part of the crew, determined them to attempt to quit the ship, and take refuge in the John as soon as she should attempt to leave us. I was confident, through the information I had received, that unless the assistance of the John were secured, the Esk, after all the labour bestowed on her, and the progress which had been made towards her preservation, must yet be abandoned as a wreck. At length, I yielded to the request of my whole crew, and made a proposal to captain Jackson, who agreed on certain conditions, involving the surrender of a large proportion of our cargo, to stay by us and assist us until our arrival at some port of Shetland. The original of this contract was voluntarily signed by every individual of both ships' companies. A subsequent agreement of a more explicit kind, on the part of masters and owners of the Esk and the John, was drawn out and signed by myself and Mr. Jackson.

These agreements being fully understood and signed, the John hauled alongside of the ice, which had now opened near the Esk for the first time since the accident, and took on board the whole of our loose blubber, estimated at seventy-eight butts and fifty-eight butts, in twenty-five casks, together with half our whalebone, as agreed. Everything now went on favourably, and whilst our crew and assistants were in full and vigorous employment, I retired to seek that repose which my wearied frame stood greatly in need of. On the 5th July, assisted by all hands from the John, the stowing of the hold and the rigging of the ship were completed, and, under a moderate breeze of wind, we left the floe, but what was our astonishment and mortification to find that the ship could not be guided! The rudder had become perfectly useless, so that with the most appropriate disposition of the sails possible, and the requisite position of the helm, the ship could not be turned round, or diverted in the least from the course in which the impetus of the wind on the sails was the most naturally balanced. This was an alarming disappointment. However, as the ship was in such constant danger of being crushed in the situation where she lay, the John, with the greatest difficulty imaginable, towed us three or four miles to the eastward, into a place of comparative safety. Here we rectified our rudder, and arranged for the trimming of the ship more by the stern, to compensate in some degree for the loss of the after-keel. When these matters were completed, on account of strong wind and thick weather, we could not, without imminent danger, attempt to penetrate the compact body of ice which at this time barred our escape to the sea, and I took the advantage of the opportunity to procure a long rest. The attention of the carpenters in caulking the ceiling of the ship, together with the advantage derived from the fothering sails, had now produced an effect so considerable, that on Sunday, the 7th of July, the original leakage was found to be reduced nearly four-fifths. During an hour, in which we were engaged in Divine service, the pumps were allowed to "stand;" two and a half feet of water, which in this interval flowed into the hold, was pumped out in twenty minutes.

After various alarms and careful attention to the leakage, together with the unremitting diligence of the crew in the use of the pumps, we descried land on the 23rd of July, and approached within three or four miles of the coast of Shetland. In the evening, the John having fulfilled the articles of agreement as far as was required, we sent the twelve men belonging to her crew on board, and after receiving from them a supply of fresh water, they left us with three cheers, and the usual display of colours. We were now left to sail by ourselves; our progress was in consequence rather slow. At daylight of the 27th, we were rejoiced with a sight of our port. Knowing the flow of water to be sufficient for the ship, and there being a probability of reaching the harbour before the tide was too much fallen, we pressed towards it with every sail we could set, and having received a pilot as we approached the pier, we immediately entered the harbour, and grounded at half-past five a.m. in a place of safety.

Thus, through the peculiar favour of God, by whose influence our perseverance was stimulated, and by whose blessing our contrivances were rendered effectual, happily terminated a voyage at once hazardous, disastrous, and interesting. Men whose lives have been exposed to dangers so fearful and imminent, may reasonably be expected to be influenced by a vivid sense of the nearness of eternity, and to feel the powers of the world to come. It is the prerogative of the Christian religion, whilst it prepares men for death, to take away undue apprehensions of it; to furnish consolation of unspeakable value, when it is present; and to light up the distant and unknown future, with the peace and happiness of the hope of eternal life. To the rude and courageous mariner, as well as to the inhabitants of refined and luxurious homes, God's message is one and the same. It is suitable, and worthy of acceptation, on sea and on land, in sickness and in health, when we expect instant removal from our present temporary dwelling-place, or look forward to the activities and cares of a protracted life. To every one of us the Almighty is saying, Repent, believe, and live—promising a free and complete pardon through the death of his Son, and engaging, to those who welcome and obey his message, that they shall live under the smile of His countenance and the protection of his power.

Intelligence relative to the distressed state of the ship, and the helplessness of her situation, reached Whitby the day before us, and, in consequence of exaggerations respecting the loss of the crew, involved every interested person in deep distress. Throughout the town, and in a great measure throughout the neighbourhood, the event was considered as a general calamity. Some of the underwriters on the Esk, I was informed, had offered sixty per cent. for the reassurance of the sums for which they were liable, but such was the nature of the risk, as ascertained from the information of some ships' crews, by whom we had been assisted, that no one would undertake the assurance, even at this extraordinary premium. The hearty congratulations I received on landing, from every acquaintance, were almost overwhelming, and these, with the enhanced endearments of my affectionate and enraptured wife, amply repaid for all the toils and anxieties of mind that I had endured.

On the tide ebbing out, the Esk was left dry, on which, for the first time since the accident, the whole of the water was drawn out of the hold by the pumps. The next tide, the ship was removed above the bridge to a place of perfect safety, where the pumps being neglected, the water in the course of two tides rose nearly as high within as without. After the cargo was discharged, the ship was put into dock, and it was found that, excepting the loss of twenty-two feet of keel, and the removal of a piece of the starboard garboard strake, nine feet in length, with a portion of dead-wood brought home upon deck, no other damage of consequence had been produced by the ice. The whole expense of repairs did not, I believe, exceed £200. Though the sacrifice of nearly one-half of our cargo was a considerable disappointment to the owners, who had been apprized of our success in fishery, yet, when compared with the salvage, which might have been demanded had no contract been entered into for the assistance of the John, the sacrifice appeared to have been a material benefit, having been productive of the saving of perhaps £2,000. The approbation of my conduct by the owners, Messrs. Fishburn and Brodrick, was testified by their presenting to me a gratuity of £50; and the sense entertained by the Whitby underwriters, of the preservation of the ship, was pleasingly manifested by a present of a handsome piece of plate.

I may add, in conclusion, that the whole of my crew, excepting one individual, returned from this adventurous and trying voyage in safety, and in general in a good state of health. Several of the men, indeed, were affected more or less by the excessive fatigue, and by the painful exposure to cold and damp, while resting on the ice; but all of them were, in a great measure, restored before our arrival at home, excepting one man; he, poor fellow, being of a weak constitution, suffered severely from the inclement exposure, and died soon after he arrived in port.